Mark Twain

Young Writer

By Miriam E. Mason

Aladdin Paperbacks

Aladdin Paperbacks
An imprint of Simon & Schuster
Children's Publishing Division
1230 Avenue of the Americas
New York, NY 10020
Copyright © 1942, 1962 by the Bobbs-Merrill Company, Inc.
All rights reserved including the right of reproduction
in whole or in part in any form.
First Aladdin Paperbacks edition, 1991

Printed in the United States of America

8   9   10

Library of Congress Cataloging-in-Publication Data

Mason, Miriam Evangeline, 1899–
    Mark Twain, boy of old Missouri / by Miriam E. Mason ; illustrated by Henry S. Gillette. — 1st Aladdin Books ed.
        p.   cm. — (The Childhood of famous Americans series)
    Summary: Describes the boyhood of Samuel Clemens in Missouri and how he came to begin a writing career under the pen name Mark Twain.
    ISBN 0-689-71480-7
    1. Twain, Mark, 1835–1910—Biography—Youth—Juvenile literature.
2. Authors, American—19th century—Biography—Juvenile literature.
3. Missouri—Social life and customs—Juvenile literature.
[1. Twain, Mark, 1835–1910—Childhood and youth.   2. Authors.
American.]   I. Gillette, Henry S., ill.   II. Title.   III. Series.
PS1332.M37   1991
818'.409—dc20
[92]
[B]   90-23768   CIP   AC

Mark Twain

Young Writer

Illustrated by Henry S. Gillette

For my three special boys
Alan, Andy, and Jimmy

Illustrations

Full pages

Numerous smaller illustrations

Contents

⋆ Mark Twain

Young Writer

Where Is Sammy?

"SAMMY, oh Sammy!" called Pamela Clemens. "Where are you? We're going home now!"

Pamela stood on tiptoe and put her hands to her mouth to make her voice louder. Margaret and Benjamin added their voices to their big sister's. Baby Henry, waking from his nap, did his share.

"Sam-m-m-y. Come on, Sammy!" they chimed.

Only a lazy river bird answered with his loud cry. No little brother appeared through the willow trees. Pamela sighed.

"I'll have to go hunt Sammy," she told the other children. "Stay here till I come back."

Pamela had brought the younger children down to the shady bank of Salt River for a picnic. It was a warm day in the spring of 1839. Sammy had slipped away from the others while Pamela was busy with her quilt piecing.

Pamela was not worried, though, as she made her way through the tall river grass. She was pretty sure where she would find Sammy. He would be just as close to the river as he could get without falling in.

She looked behind a curtain of willow branches and there, sure enough, was Sammy. He was sitting on a log that hung part way out over the shining water.

"I didn't hear you!" said Sammy when his big sister scolded him. "Oh dear!" he sighed, "do we have to leave the river?"

"It's nearly suppertime," answered Pamela, helping Sammy down from the log. "Mother will be looking for us."

Sammy Clemens was four years old. He was a thin little boy with sandy curls, bright mischievous eyes, and a mouth that was usually laughing or singing.

"I think a river is the nicest place in the world," said Sammy. He looked back for one last glimpse of the gleaming water.

Pamela laughed. "It's too bad you couldn't have been a duck or a fish," she said. "You would have been so happy!"

Soon the children left the cool riverside and were on their way back to the dusty little village where they lived. The name of the village was Florida. The town, which was located in the new state of Missouri, looked like many other pioneer villages of the time.

"I think Salt River is a prettier town than Florida," said Sammy, kicking up the deep dust with his bare feet.

"At least it's not dusty," said Margaret.

Mother had supper on the table when the children returned from the picnic. Mother's name was Jane. She was a pretty woman—full of fun and jokes.

Mr. Clemens was a lawyer, and he did not find much work in that pioneer village. He was a tall, pale man who did not smile often though he was very kind-hearted.

Orion was the oldest boy of the family, and Pamela was the oldest girl. Margaret and Benjamin and Sammy came next. Last of all was Henry, the baby.

Mother had cheerful news for them as they sat down to the table. "There is going to be a house-raising for Hugh Hickman's boy," she said. "Aunt Patsey wants us all to go."

"A house-raising!" the children exclaimed together. "What fun!"

"Will the house-raising be down by the river?" asked Sammy. "If I had a house I'd want it to be right next to the river so that I could see the river, smell the river, and hear the river all day and all night!"

Pamela laughed. "You funny little mop top, Sammy." She rumpled his thick flaxen hair. "The Salt River isn't so much. Why, it's hardly more than a creek!"

THE HOUSE-RAISING

"Goody, goody, goody, we're going to a house-raising!" sang Sammy in an excited voice, as he rushed around the kitchen where the family was getting ready for the big picnic.

In those days when a young couple got married, or a new family came to live in the town, the people had a house-raising for them.

A house-raising was really a big work picnic. The women took along great baskets of food. The men rolled logs and built the new house.

15

The children played and everybody had fun. It did not take long to raise the log house.

The Clemens kitchen was a busy place. The slave girl, Jennie, was frying big platters of chicken and pork. Pamela and Mother were baking dried-apple pies.

Orion had gathered roasting ears from the cornfield early that morning.

Sammy nearly ran into Jennie who was carrying a large platter of fried chicken.

"I'm sorry, Jennie," said Sammy.

"You take care of the baby, Sammy," said his mother. "Take him outside for a while."

Sammy took his baby brother outside and sang to him. He could hardly wait until time to start. The house-raising would be down by the river. That made the event all the nicer.

"Down by the river, the bright shining river," Sammy sang to Henry.

All the families for miles around came to help

with the house-raising. At dusk a new little log house was standing among the tree stumps above the river.

Then the men built a great fire from the left-over logs and branches. Everybody sat around the red flames, resting from their work, while they drank cider and sang or talked.

They sang a jolly old pioneer song which Sammy liked:

"My name it is Joe Bowers,
    I've got a brother Ike.
I came from old Missouri.
    Yes, all the way from Pike!"

"I come from old Missouri," sang little Sammy in a high bright voice.

The songs of the frogs and the crickets and the river birds seemed to mix with the voices of the people into one big sleepy song.

The night smells were sleepy and pleasant—wood smoke, marshy riverbank, damp forest.

"I like the river," whispered Sammy. He went to sleep against his mother's shoulder. The house-raising was over.

The people in the tiny settlement would talk about the house-raising for days. Whenever a new home was built the people were hopeful.

"Someday I am sure the town will be big and prosperous," said Mr. Clemens. "Then there will be more work for a lawyer."

A New Dress for Mother

"WE MUST all have new clothes," said Mother happily, as she went with the children to Uncle John's store. "The town is growing. A new church has been built and there will be Sunday school every Sunday."

"It will seem more like a real town when we have a church here," said Pamela.

Pamela was going to be the organist.

The Clemens children loved to go to Uncle John's store. Uncle John was friendly and jolly. His store was filled with interesting things. He always gave them something each time they visited his store.

19

Today he gave the children a big handful of crackers from the barrel which had just been opened. Then he got out the big rolls of bright new calico which he had brought from St. Louis the week before.

"I want something with pink and green flowers," said Pamela eagerly. Her uncle had just what she was looking for.

"And what for the little ones?" he asked kindly. "Some nice blue, or brown?"

"Something as near the color of mud as you have," answered Mother in a joking voice. Mrs. Clemens picked out a pretty blue for Benjamin and a calico with white stars on a black background for Margaret. She chose a bright yellow with red rosebuds for baby Henry.

"This is the prettiest fabric I have," said Uncle John as he got out another roll. He unfolded a bolt of bright striped material for Mrs. Clemens to see. It was beautiful.

"You should have a striped dress, Jane," he said. "You like stripes so well."

Mother looked at the pretty calico longingly, but shook her head.

"It is much too bright and gaudy for a backwoods mother," she replied. "Show me something darker, please."

In the meantime Sammy had been walking around the store looking at everything. He nearly fell into a barrel of fish. He had knocked down some tools which barely missed his head. He was about to reach into a barrel of brown sugar, when he noticed the striped material.

"Pretty!" he cried, forgetting all about the sugar. He stood on tiptoe and tried to reach the fabric. "Pretty!"

Uncle John got out a dark calico material with small stars in it.

"I will take five yards of that material, John," said Mrs. Clemens.

Sammy began to cry. He cried so loudly that his mother was alarmed. "Did a bee sting you, Sammy?" she asked.

Sammy pointed to the bright striped fabric. His hazel eyes flashed. His sandy curls flew out as he shook his head violently.

"Pretty!" he repeated. He pushed the dark calico away. "No!"

"I ought to spank you," Mrs. Clemens laughed.

"Oh, Mother, get the striped calico," urged Pamela. "You can still spank Sammy if you want to," she added. "You can always find a reason for doing that!"

When the new Sunday school started, all the members of the Clemens family were present in their new clothes. John and Orion and Benjamin were wearing new shirts of neat, clear blue. Pamela looked like a rose with her rosy cheeks and black hair. She was wearing her flowered pink dress. Little Margaret looked like a Christmas tree doll dressed in black spangled with white stars.

Handsomest and brightest of all were Sammy and his mother. Their new clothes were striped —beautiful bright stripes with ruffled collars just alike!

Sammy was a little disappointed in Sunday school. When the first excitement of the new place was over, he found it rather boring.

Flies and wasps came in to inspect the new building and to join in the singing. Yellow-jackets were likely to sting anyone who dozed off into a nap.

The teachers were not the best. They were likely to moralize and preach a little too much which made Sammy yawn.

Sammy liked the Bible stories. He listened fascinated to the stories of Moses, the lawgiver, and his long years of travel, as he led his people to the Promised Land. Forty years for a journey of about three hundred miles! What adventures they had along the way!

The frontier child was spellbound by the story of the great lawgiver's burial. In a community where funerals were rather important affairs with weeping and wailing, such a burial was hardly believable.

"He just went up on a mountain and died and the Lord Himself buried him and nobody ever knew where the grave was," Sammy repeated this thrilling story to Uncle Ned, the man of all work, when he went home.

The New Testament stories were interesting, too. Sammy liked the simple, beautiful sound of the words. Many of those words wrote themselves in his mind forever.

Galilee, the Sea of Galilee, Palestine, Jordan, Jerusalem, Smyrna, were some of the words which stayed in his mind. He could hardly believe that these were real names of real places, nor that the wonderful things in the stories had really happened.

"If I went on a trip to the Holy Land could I see all those places with my very own eyes?" he asked Pamela.

"Of course," answered his older sister. "Many people travel to the Holy Land to look at the Sea of Galilee and the land of Egypt and the Mountains of Moab."

"I'd like to go there some day," declared Sammy thoughtfully. "Only I'd want a steamboat to ride on over the Sea of Galilee. I wouldn't want to take forty years to go three hundred miles. I'd make the trip in Father's carriage with a couple of fast colts."

"How you imagine things!" said Pamela lovingly.

Hannibal

"MOVING IS fun!" said Sammy as the family jogged along in the carriage. "It's like a rocking chair——"

"A rocking chair with a broken rocker!" exclaimed Pamela, as a wheel hit a hole in the road. Everyone lurched sideways.

The Clemens family was moving from the village of Florida to the town of Hannibal, Missouri. Hannibal was located on the bank of the great Mississippi River.

Things had not gone so well for Mr. Clemens in Florida. There was not enough for a lawyer to do in such a tiny village.

"In a town the size of Hannibal," said Mr. Clemens, "there should be plenty of work for a lawyer." In addition to practicing law, Sammy's father planned to operate a store. He expected to be very busy in their new home.

Mrs. Clemens was glad to leave Florida, too. She was certain that she would enjoy living in a bigger town.

One of the Clemens children did not go with the family to Hannibal. Little Margaret had fallen ill a few weeks before and died. So now there were five children instead of six.

Sammy missed Margaret. He wished that she could be riding along the road to Hannibal with the rest of them.

"But never mind, Goldie," said Sammy to the cat. Goldie and her kittens were riding in a covered basket on Sammy's lap. "I promise to look after you and all your children."

Hearing Sammy's voice, Goldie mewed plaintively. She did not like traveling in a covered basket over bumpy mud roads. Especially, she did not like it when she had five kittens to look after.

Goldie had been the special pet of Margaret and Sammy. Together they had picked out names for her new born kittens.

"They must have Bible names," said the little girl who liked going to Sunday school. She and Sammy had named the kittens for the heroes of their Sunday school lessons.

"Here's Peter and there's Paul," Margaret had said. "This one is Simon. That one over there shall be called Methuselah, who lived so long."

"The striped one can be Moses," Sammy had decided, "because he looks like a leader."

It was only a week later that Margaret had died so suddenly, as children often did in those days. Her death was the first break in the family and a great sorrow to them all.

Sammy would not dream of leaving Goldie and her kittens behind. The whole family helped to settle her in the basket.

"We forgot Orion!" Sammy suddenly screamed. They were already five miles down the road. Mr. Clemens turned around and went back to get him.

Each child wanted to be the first to see the new town. Sammy tried hard to keep his eyes open, but the warm sunshine, the jogging wheels, and the quiet voices of his mother and Pamela made him sleepy. So it was Orion who first saw the little town along the riverbank.

"We're here! We're here!" called Orion. "Here's Hannibal!"

Sammy was awake in an instant. He looked ahead and rubbed his eyes. Then he gave a cry of delight and clapped his hands.

"There's a river!" he cried excitedly. "A big river! It's a giant's river!"

It was the great Mississippi River which Sammy saw. No wonder it looked like a giant's river to the small boy. The great river was a mile wide where Hannibal was located. On the opposite side, the green shores of Illinois looked like misty walls.

Sammy could tell that the Mississippi was a busy river, too—not at all like the quiet little Salt River where he had played so often. Slow flatboats floated by and some children waved at Sammy from a houseboat. Heavy rafts, loaded with lumber, seemed hardly to move as they crept along.

"I'm glad you were the first one to see the town," Sammy told his big brother. Orion was hardly ever lucky about anything.

While the children watched, they heard a harsh whistle from downriver. In a minute the Clemens children were thrilled by the sight of a steamboat splashing through the water.

"The town's waking up!" cried Sammy. He gazed with wonder toward the landing. As they approached the town it seemed to be sleeping. Now suddenly at the sound of the steamboat's whistle, people began to rush toward the river. Slaves were busy with barrels and bales. Children came flying from all directions.

"When I grow up I want to ride on a boat like that!" breathed Sammy. His eyes got bigger. "I want to run a boat like that!"

A big platform was laid from the steamboat to the shore. The captain came on deck. He was wearing a handsome uniform with many bright buttons on it. A lady and a little girl got on the boat. They were very elegant looking.

"Maybe I'll even have a steamboat of my very own someday!" dreamed Sammy aloud.

When the boat moved off with much splashing and whistle blowing, the Clemens family drove on up the street.

"I think we'll like it here," said Pamela. "Look over there. There's even a hotel!"

"This is the town square," said Father, as they drove through a grove. There were plum trees, hazel bushes, and grapevines there.

Mrs. Clemens was pleased to see that the town had several churches and a school.

"Will our house be close to the river?" asked Sammy. He could hardly take his eyes from the broad shining waters of the Mississippi.

"Not too close, I hope," his mother smiled. "I'll have other things to do besides pulling you out of the water three times a day!"

The new house was a plain little building on Bird Street, but the family was pleased with it.

To Sammy's delight there was a good view of the river with its boats and barges. He could also see Bear Creek, which was a baby-sized river.

A mile behind the town the tall trees of a

forest stood like dark and silent Indians. There was a high hill near their new home. Anyone who stood on the hill could see for miles around.

Sammy liked nearly everything about Hannibal, but most of all he liked the river. At every possible opportunity he would go like a bird from a cage in the direction of the great Mississippi.

There he would sit and stare at the slowly moving water, the misty shores of Illinois, the magnificent packet boats riding the current.

"He drives me crazy!" his mother often cried in exasperation. "He gives me more worry than all the other children put together!"

Mrs. Clemens lived in dread lest her runaway child be carried home from the river one day, limp and lifeless as a drowned cat. But Sammy lived on in spite of the risks and dangers. The family began to feel at home in Hannibal.

Helpful Sammy

It was a busy day for the Clemens family. Mrs. Clemens and Pamela were making the house look its very best. Jennie was in the kitchen baking pies and cakes. Tomorrow the preacher was coming to their house for dinner.

"Let me go to the store with you today," Sammy begged his father. "I'll help sell things."

Mr. Clemens and Orion were on their way to open the store for the day. Mr. Clemens shook his head in his gentle, unsmiling way. "You stay home and help Mother, Sammy," he replied.

"You'd be sure to fall in the pickle barrel," added Orion. "Then you would be lost for good because we wouldn't be able to tell you from the other pickles."

Sammy wandered about aimlessly. He really did want to be helpful. Mrs. Clemens came into the kitchen just as Sammy was starting to break some eggs into the piecrust bowl.

"I want to help," said Sammy.

"You can help by playing with Henry," said his mother. "Why don't you take him outside?" She lifted the baby from his trundle bed.

"I'll take Henry for a ride," said Sammy, as he helped Henry into the homemade wagon. He went down the street pulling the wagon. Henry laughed and shouted happily.

"Here comes a steamboat!" called Sammy. He held up his head and made a puffing, hissing noise. "Here comes a great, big steamboat on the Memphis line!"

"Get up! Get up there!" called Henry. He thought this was a game of horse.

Sammy's thoughts were not of horses or slow oxen. He was making believe that the dusty street was the wide, shining river and that the clumsy little wagon was a huge, shining steamboat. Sammy was the steamboat pilot, and the captain, and the crew all in one.

Henry was a passenger—a rich man going to New Orleans.

"Toot! Too-oot! Too-oo-oot!" cried Sammy going toward the river. "Half twain, quarter twain, mark twain!"

He had often listened to the rivermen measuring the water with a sounding line. He knew what the river call meant.

"Mark twain" meant safe water—water deep enough to hold up the boat. It was a good sound for a boatman to hear.

When Sammy came closer to the river he noticed that something very interesting was going on near one of the boats.

Sammy often watched the boats as they were being loaded with hemp and lard and timber. He stopped to watch the black slaves roll barrels and bales. He loved to hear them sing as they often did as they worked.

Today he watched as a strange load was being transferred from one boat to another. It was a boatload of black men who were being sent to New Orleans.

These men were not singing. They were sad and quiet. They weren't working either. They were all fastened together with a chain.

"Where are those men going?" Sammy asked an old riverman who was standing nearby. When the old man explained to him what was happening, tears ran down Sammy's cheeks.

"It's not fair!" said Sammy angrily. It's not fair for them to be fastened together like that! They can't go where they want to, or do what they want to do!"

"They are slaves," said the old man. "It's a sad thing to be a slave, sonny. Some day we won't have any slaves in this country. You wait and see. When you're as old as I am, the blacks won't be slaves anymore!"

Sammy hoped this was true. He liked Jennie and the other slaves who were so friendly to him. He wanted them to be happy.

The kind-hearted old boatman picked Sammy up in his arms so he could see better. Sammy had forgotten about Henry, sitting patiently in his little wagon up the street.

"Where do so many boats come from?" he asked the old man.

"They come from the Illinois River and the Red River, from the White River and the Missouri, from the Upper Mississippi and the Ohio," the man replied. "They come from the Monongahela and the Tennessee, the Cumberland and the Arkansas and the Yazoo!"

"Say it again. Say it again!" cried Sammy in delight. It sounded like a song to him.

The old riverman was glad to talk to such a good listener. He said the names over and over. Sammy said them after him again. He pointed out the different boats on the river and told Sammy what kind of boats they were.

Sammy was astonished when Jennie suddenly appeared, looking angry and frightened.

"It's a long past dinnertime. Your mamma was afraid you and baby Henry had gone down to the bottom of the river!" scolded Jennie.

Together they went in search of Henry. They found him sound asleep in his wagon—dried-up tears on his cheeks. Jennie scolded Sammy again.

"Anyway I helped," said Sammy. "I took care of Henry while you got ready for the preacher, didn't I?" he demanded. He went home whispering the river names over and over to himself.

Sammy liked the sound of names because they were interesting words. He had a taste for words, just as Goldie had a taste for mice.

"Hannibal! Hannibal!" murmured Sammy. That was a word that rolled, like marbles on the ground. Mississippi was a big proud word that sounded like what it meant—the Father of Waters.

Even Bear Creek reminded Sammy of bears —big, dark, furry bears.

ADVENTURE IN BEAR CREEK

"Are there any bears in Bear Creek?" wondered Sammy. He often sat in the top of the big apple tree and looked down at the creek. It seemed very tiny, hardly big enough for bears to hide in.

"But if there are bears down there," he thought, "and if I went down there with my bow and arrow, I might kill some like Daniel Boone used to do."

Mrs. Clemens often told Sammy stories about the famous woodsman Daniel Boone.

"If I killed a few bears," he thought, "I could skin them and sell the skins. With the money I could buy myself a steamboat!"

Mr. Clemens didn't think there were any bears left in or near Bear Creek.

"If any cows are there," said Orion, "they will eat you up with the other green stuff."

Sammy was not frightened by Orion's grim words. He knew that Orion was only joking and that his big brother loved him dearly.

The apple tree made a good hiding place for Sammy. He could be alone there, just thinking and dreaming and looking.

Sometimes Goldie and her kittens would scramble up the tree and stretch out near Sammy. He didn't mind this for they were quiet companions. They did not scold or preach or remind him that his face was dirty.

"Do you reckon there's bears along Bear Creek, Goldie?" he asked one day. Goldie remained silent, her tail twitching and her green eyes wise.

"I'm going to find out," Sammy decided suddenly. "I'm going to find out right now! If I get a bear, Goldie, the liver's for you."

When Sammy made up his mind to do something, he wanted to do it right away.

"He acts first and thinks afterwards!" his mother often said.

Sammy slid down the tree, slingshot in hand. He headed for Bear Creek.

"Maybe you ain't a big river, but you've got a big river smell," he said to the willow-shaded water.

Sammy walked boldly into the shade of the trees, his slingshot ready for any wild animals.

After the bright sunlight and the dusty road, the shade and grass felt cool and pleasant to his bare head and his small dusty feet.

Though Sammy looked about carefully, he could see no bears. Nor did he see any bear tracks on the ground. He hid behind a willow tree for several moments, silently pretending to be Daniel Boone. Still no bears appeared.

Sammy hardly knew whether to be pleased or disappointed. He knew that it would be a pretty scary thing to meet a bear and fight him with a slingshot. One thing was certain, though, if he did just that, he would have something to talk about for the rest of his life!

A sudden splashing sound made Sammy jump. "Shucks, it's only frogs!" he realized.

The frogs croaked in deep voices, "Ar-ump, ar-ump!" Sammy giggled. He thought the frogs sounded exactly like the preacher when he cleared his throat before giving out the hymn.

"Mother would like some good fried frog legs," he thought. "She'd like them almost as well as bear steaks, maybe. She might even like them better than bear steaks!"

Sammy crept to the creek bank and waited for the frogs to come up. When a big one appeared he took careful aim with his slingshot.

There was a sudden shower of water drops and a startled water-soaked howl. However, it was not a frog that made the splash. Nor was it a frog that cried, "Help! Help! Help!"

Sammy had been so interested in the frog shooting that he forgot to watch where he was going. He went head first into the creek.

The water was deep and Sammy had not yet learned how to swim. He caught on to an old willow stump sticking up from the water. He managed to perch there, but he was out of reach of the creek bank. The water was too deep for him to wade.

"If I just had a boat it'd be easy to get home," he thought mournfully, clinging to the uncomfortable stump. "If I could just've killed a bear, I might have enough money to buy a boat!"

As luck would have it, some slave boys in a boat came by before Sammy fell back into the water.

"We almost about didn't stop," said one of the boys, after they had helped the damp and weary Sammy into their boat.

"We thought sure when we heard you holler that it was the ghosties," the other boy added. "If we hadn't had on our charms against ha'nts, we'd have been afraid to stop."

Sammy rode to shore with his new friends. He hadn't caught a bear. He hadn't even seen a bear. He wasn't really any nearer the answer to his question than he had been before he came. But he had had his adventure in Bear Creek. Sammy was to be fished out of that creek at least sixteen times before he was twelve years old.

As he thought over his adventure, it took on a sort of shine and glow. It really hadn't been fun when he was clinging to the willow stump, wondering how long he could hold out. He hoped he wouldn't be that near Heaven again for a long time.

All the same, when he was up in the apple tree, or tucked into his bed at night, or sitting in front of the fireplace, Sammy enjoyed thinking of his adventure on Bear Creek.

He enjoyed talking about it, too. The adventure grew a tiny bit larger with each telling. Sometimes Sammy even told his adventure story to his friends at the river landing.

Many of the rivermen and workers down there knew the wiry little towhead and welcomed his company. If they were not too busy, they would listen admiringly to his tale of the great frogs, the dangerous water, and his timely rescue.

"What do you know!" an old riverman might say wistfully, "You're certainly a lad cut out for adventure!"

Schoolboy

"SAMMY NEEDS something to do," said John Clemens sternly. "He spends too much time at the landing talking to the rivermen."

"If he's not down by the river," sighed Mrs. Clemens, "he's down by Bear Creek. It's a wonder he hasn't drowned, but he's too little to work, John."

"Why can't Sammy go to school?" Pamela asked. "That would give him something to do every day, and it wouldn't be too hard."

Mr. Clemens nodded. "I believe Pamela is right, Mother. Perhaps Sammy would not always be getting into mischief if he were in school."

Mr. and Mrs. Clemens could not understand why Sammy was always running down to the river or the creek. They were afraid he might grow up to be an idler, or a tramp, or even a lazy riverman.

"Mrs. Horr would like Sammy to come to school with me," said Pamela one day.

"It costs twenty-five cents a week," sighed Mrs. Clemens. "That's quite a lot of money, but I guess it would be worth it just to get Sammy out from under foot for a while."

Sammy didn't want to go to school at all. "I'll be good," he promised. "I'll be terrible good if you won't make me go to school. I'll not run away any more. I'll not fall in the river. I'll take good care of the baby."

"You're five years old, Sammy," said his father sternly. "You're old enough to go to school. You must have an education."

Pamela went to Mrs. Horr's school and loved

it. She was one of the teacher's best pupils. She won many prizes for her good work.

"You'll like it," she said to her little brother, as she led him to school the first morning.

Sammy lagged behind his sister. He felt gloomy. He was cleaned and scrubbed. His light curls were brushed and combed. He wore a clean, starched shirt, but he was very unhappy.

"So this is dear little Sammy!" chirped Mrs. Horr. Sammy stared at her. She had stiff little curls all around her plump face and she wore a black silk apron over her dress.

"I won't like her!" thought Sammy to himself. "I won't like her a bit. I'd lots rather stay home with Jennie!"

School was the same every day. First there was a prayer, then a chapter was read from the Bible. After that, Mrs. Horr read the rules of the school. She read them every day. They were very strict rules.

"There will be no playing or idling on the way to school," she read. "There will be no shouting, no yelling, no quarreling or fighting.

"Children who do not know their lessons," she went on, "will be switched. Children who dawdle or do not pay attention will be switched."

"I don't like school!" declared Sammy.

On Fridays they had speech. Next they had spelling lessons. Next the children had to give recitations. Pamela was nearly always chosen to speak because she did so well.

"I can sing," thought Sammy. "I can sing the song about Ike Bowers."

Mrs. Horr would not let Sammy sing the song. Instead she made him recite a silly little poem.

"You'd scarce expect one of my age
To speak in public on the stage."

On warm days it was harder than ever for

Sammy to pay attention in class. One day Mrs. Horr became very angry at him.

"Samuel Langhorne Clemens!" she cried in her high, scolding voice, which sounded like a sparrow's voice. "You deserve to be punished. You shall be switched!"

All the children looked frightened. Mrs. Horr reached around for her switch, but she could not find it. This made her even angrier, so she thought she would punish Sammy a little more.

"Samuel Clemens," the teacher said grimly. "You may go outside and get a switch. And get a good strong one!"

Sammy went out into the sunshine. There were all kinds of trees around—oak trees, maple trees, hazel bushes, and plum trees. There were dozens and hundreds of switches. Sammy hardly knew which one to choose.

He walked on down the street till he came to the cooper's shop at the foot of the hill. In the yard were many tiny shavings which looked like golden curls. Sammy chose a dainty little shaving a few inches long.

"This will make a fine switch," he thought. "Here is the best switch I could find, ma'am!" said Sammy, handing the shaving to the teacher.

The children began to laugh. Mrs. Horr looked very angry. Her fat face got redder and redder. Her stiff little curls got stiffer.

"I will teach you to play jokes on me!" she cried. She laid Sammy across her knee and spanked him. Dust flew in clouds from his trousers. Tears fell in streams from his eyes.

Sammy felt this was one of the most unhappy days of his life. He wished he could grow up into an Indian and get Mrs. Horr's scalp.

The day had its bright side after all. Sammy's mother never sent him back to Mrs. Horr's school again. Getting away from school was certainly worth two spankings to Sammy.

Summer with Uncle John

SAMMY KNEW his father and mother were thinking about something. He felt sure it was something about him. He could tell by the way they acted—as if they had a secret. Sometimes he would hear bits of sentences in low tones.

"I think it would be a good thing," said Mr. Clemens to his wife one day.

"Perhaps it would, John," replied Mrs. Clemens, "but Sammy is so little. What if he should get sick?"

Sammy was worried about the whispering and wondering. He wondered what it was all about.

It might be something about school. If it was,

then no wonder his parents looked so serious. Sammy hadn't done well in school—not at all like Pamela, who won prizes and honors.

Maybe they were afraid he was going to die. Sammy didn't like that idea, but then he wasn't very well. After he had fallen into the creek the last time, he kept his wet clothes on a long time. That gave him a bad cold.

Perhaps his parents were going to have the steam doctor come to work on him. The steam doctor was a very up-to-date doctor who traveled all about the country trying out a new steam cure on sick people.

Sammy felt that he would rather be sick than steamed and scalded like one of the chickens that Jennie cooked! He had nothing to worry about though. His parents' secret proved to be a very happy one.

"Your Uncle John is coming to town tomorrow," his mother told him. "He and Aunt Patsey want you to go home with them. Do you think you would like that, Sammy? Do you think you would get homesick? After all, you're quite a big boy now—nearly six——"

"What time will Uncle John get here?" Sammy interrupted. "How soon can we go? How long can I stay with them?"

Sammy could hardly wait. He rushed to his room to pack so that he would not keep Uncle John waiting the next day. He could hardly close his eyes that night. When he finally did go to sleep he walked in his dreams.

"I'm on my way to Uncle John's house!" he said drowsily. His mother caught Sammy walking like a little ghost in his nightgown in the middle of the night.

Of course, there were a few bad moments the next morning when Sammy turned to say good-by to his family. His nose and eyes felt funny. He kept having to wipe his eyes.

Sammy soon felt better as he rode along beside jolly Mr. Quarles and listened to the good stories which his uncle told him.

The miles passed as they jogged along the bumpy Salt River road.

"There's the house we helped raise for the Hickmans!" Sammy cried, looking at the log house by the riverbank. There were vines over the doorway now and a yellow rosebush in the yard. The bare cabin had turned into a home.

A little farther on Sammy saw Uncle John's house. It looked even nicer than he had remembered, with pink and yellow roses in the yard and an orchard behind the house.

Sammy stood up, nearly falling out of the wagon in his excitement. "We're here, we're here, we're here!" he called.

Old Shep, the dog, heard the rattle of wagon wheels and gave a sharp welcoming bark. He came racing down the road to meet his master.

At the sound of the dog's glad bark Uncle John's children came running to meet them. Aunt Patsey stood smiling in the doorway.

"My, you've grown!" she greeted her nephew. She lifted him down from the wagon and kissed him heartily. "You're so thin. We'll have to fatten you up before you go home!"

A good smell came from inside the house. Sammy saw a big table spread with delicious looking food. The table was in the roofed hallway between the two halves of the double house. It was the summertime dining room. He remembered that it was always cool and pleasant there.

Aunt Patsey's table was always well supplied with good food, but this evening there was more food than ever in Sammy's honor.

"What are you whispering to yourself?" his cousin Nancy asked Sammy while they were eating. "You keep whispering something and counting on your fingers. Are you saying a charm?"

"I'm trying to think of all the good things to eat I've ever seen on this table," said Sammy. He looked a little provoked. "You bothered me, too. Now I've got to begin all over!"

He began to list aloud the things which he had been counting up in his mind. "Fried chicken, roast pig, wild turkey, tame turkey, ducks, geese, squirrel, rabbit, venison——"

"Frog legs," chimed in Nancy. "Prairie chicken, and baked possum."

"Biscuits, corn pone, buckwheat cakes, corn on the ear," added little John. "Beans, and peas, and turnips, and potatoes, and yams."

"Apple pie, watermelons, cantaloupe, peach cobbler, tree molasses," Sammy went on.

"Don't forget sauerkraut," said Aunt Patsey. She was proud of her homemade sauerkraut.

"What about my fine hickory-smoked hams, and stuffed sausages, and scrapple?" added Uncle John.

Sammy closed his eyes and remembered summer mornings and cool autumn evenings. "Strawberries, 'n' blackberries, 'n' wild grapes, 'n' pawpaws, 'n' persimmons 'n' hickory nuts, 'n' hazelnuts, 'n', 'n'——"

"That's a-plenty," laughed Aunt Patsey. "Already I feel like a fattening hog myself. If you name any more foods I'll have to bring out the pain-killer!"

Sammy went to bed early that night. He was very tired after his trip and the excitement of the day. How pleasant and familiar it seemed to go up the stairway to the attic bedroom he would share with little John and Cy.

Moonlight came in through the window and made squares on the bed. Sammy felt peaceful and sad and happy all at once. It was nice to be back at Uncle John's house, but he hoped that everybody at home was well and happy. He was sorry he had not done better in school and won at least one prize card. He wished he had looked after baby Henry more carefully.

"When I go back home, I'll wash my face and hands cleaner before I start to Sunday school, too," he thought as he drifted off to sleep.

OLD AUNT HANNA

Sunshine poured through the bedroom window, but Sammy was wide-awake. He did not have to wait for it to say, "Get up!"

"What are you going to do first today, Sammy?" asked Aunt Patsey gaily, as Sammy ate his breakfast.

"I want to go see Aunt Hanna," answered Sammy eagerly. He could hardly take time to eat the delicious breakfast before him.

Aunt Hanna was one of Uncle John's slaves. She lived in one of the little houses behind the orchard near the tobacco fields.

She was an old, old lady—so old that nobody knew just how many years she had lived. Aunt Hanna knew magic charms of all kinds. She could tell endless stories about ghosts and goblins and ha'nts. She loved children and all the children loved her, too.

Aunt Patsey gave Sammy a bowl of custard to take to Aunt Hanna who was rather feeble. She had to stay in bed most of the time.

His cousins Nancy and Cy and Little John went with Sammy. The children walked past the garden, through the orchard to the tobacco fields where little clusters of white-washed houses stood.

"I wonder how old Aunt Hanna is," said Sammy aloud, as he thought of the tiny, wrinkled old woman.

"Oh, she's terrible old," answered Nancy. "She's two or three hundred years old! She remembers Moses when he was a tiny baby."

"Moses lived hundreds of years ago," said John, thinking over his Bible stories. "Moses lived before Jesus was born."

"Why that's more than eighteen hundred years ago!" said Cy.

Sammy's eyes opened wide.

"Then Aunt Hanna is more than eighteen hundred years old," he said admiringly. "My, I wonder if I'll ever be that old!"

"Course not," returned Cy. "You're just an ordinary boy, like us. Aunt Hanna knows all about charms and witches and things. That's why she's lived so long."

"I do hope Aunt Hanna will tell us some more about how she used to play with baby Moses down by the bulrush trees," said Sammy.

When the children arrived Aunt Hanna was propped up in bed. Her kindly face was like a wrinkled-up coffee berry. Her hair was as white as the inside of a dried milkweed pod.

"I knew you'd come," she told Sammy. "The spirits told me last week you'd be here today!" Sammy brought the bowl of custard over to the bed and gave it to the old woman.

"Do you still remember when Moses was a little baby?" he asked eagerly. Aunt Hanna nodded her white head.

"Plain as yesterday," she replied. "Moses was a good little boy. He lived in a little house under the bulrush trees. All day long he played his little harp for old King Saul——"

"Wasn't it David who played the harp, Aunt Hanna?" asked Nancy anxiously.

"Maybe it was and maybe it wasn't," said the old woman, beginning to eat the custard.

Sammy waited till Aunt Hanna had finished eating before he asked the favor he wished.

"I want to take a present to Mother when I go home," he said. "I want it to be an extra nice present—something special."

"That's a good boy," mumbled Aunt Hanna. "You're good to think of your mother. What do you want for her?"

"I thought I'd like to take her one of your

68

charms," said Sammy eagerly. "I'd like to take her an extra good charm against witches. Will you make one for me?"

"Sure!" Aunt Hanna replied. "You get me a big buckeye nut by moonlight and bring it to me. I'll make a charm against witches, goblins, ghosts, and the evil eye!"

Sammy felt happy. A good charm like that would be a nice thing for his mother to have. It might make up to her for some of the things he had done—such as running away, falling into the water, and idling in school.

"You're a good friend to have, Aunt Hanna!" Sammy exclaimed.

"I'll make you a charm for your sister Pamela, too," promised Aunt Hanna. "I'll make her a love charm. It'll get her a nice sweetheart."

"That'll be fine," replied Sammy happily. Pamela was so sweet and kind and pretty. A love charm would be just what she deserved!

Sammy had a toothache. It had started the day before, just after he had finished chewing a big piece of tree sugar. It kept on hurting and the pain wouldn't go away.

"It nags and pokes just like Mrs. Horr used to do with her ruler," he thought. He went to bed early that night, but he couldn't sleep.

This morning, although Aunt Patsey had a good breakfast of ham and eggs, hot biscuits and tree molasses, he didn't feel like eating.

Aunt Patsey looked at him kindly. "We'll soon fix that tooth," she said in her cheery way.

"I've got a big bottle of pain-killer here," she went on, "that I bought from the traveling medicine man last year. It will kill that pain just as you'd kill a mosquito."

Aunt Patsey took down the big brown bottle from the pantry shelf which the medicine man had sold to her for a dollar.

70

"It smells pretty dreadful!" said Sammy. "It smells hot. Maybe I'd better just keep the toothache, Aunt Patsey."

"Stuff and nonsense!" his aunt replied cheerfully. She poured some of the dark brown medicine on a little piece of cotton. "Now, Sammy, open your mouth wide!"

Sammy bravely did as he was told. The painkiller was hotter than anything he had ever put in his mouth. Sammy's eyes got bigger and bigger with surprise and pain, as the burning medicine ran over his tongue.

"Is it better?" asked his cousins. They had been watching with keen interest.

"It's—it's kind of spread the pain all over," Sammy answered. Tears rolled down his cheeks. "It's awful hot. I think it sort of burns out the pain, don't you, Aunt Patsey?"

Noon came and Sammy's tooth still ached. Aunt Patsey decided to try something else.

"We'll go to the woods and hunt some herbs," she said briskly. "I might have known that patent medicine was no good. I can cure that pain myself a lot quicker!"

Aunt Patsey got the herb basket and set out for the woods. Sammy and the other children followed close behind her.

The woods were cool and dim, with a damp sweet smell. Sammy scuffed along through the soft old leaves which had fallen year after year and were never raked up.

Now and then they came to a patch of Indian paintbrush flowers growing tall and glowing crimson in the dimness. Wild grapevines hung thick in some of the trees.

Sammy took deep breaths and felt better. "There's no perfume in the world sweeter than the perfume of wild grape blossoms," he said.

"You rest here awhile," Aunt Patsey instructed Sammy.

Sammy stretched out on some soft velvety moss and looked up through the treetops. He noticed how the sky looked like a pale blue and white lace pattern.

"Heaven must be a little bit like the woods," Sammy said to John, who was sitting near by. He thought for a minute and added, "But I'd a lot rather go to the woods than go to heaven!"

The trees shook their leaves gently. They reminded Sammy of the way his mother sometimes shook her head at him.

Nearby, a woodpecker hammered at an old oak tree. In the distance pheasants drummed without stopping. Little John went to sleep, and did not wake even when a teasing squirrel dropped a beechnut right on his nose.

"Next to the river, the woods is the nicest place in the world," thought Sammy dreamily.

In a little while Aunt Patsey and his cousins returned. Aunt Patsey had a basket of herbs. Cy was carrying a big round hornets' nest from which the hornets had moved. Nancy's hands were filled with wild flowers.

"It's going to rain, and we'd better hurry," said his aunt. "It won't help that toothache any for you to get wet!"

"Why!" Sammy stopped suddenly and put his hand to his jaw. "It's gone. The pain is all gone! Even the pain-killer pain is gone!"

"And after I walked the woods over to find just the right herbs for a toothache!" laughed Aunt Patsey. "Maybe that pain-killer was worth more than we thought!"

"It wasn't the pain-killer," replied Sammy. "It was the cool green woods."

All his life long Sammy loved this woods—the deep shadows, the wild flowers, the smells of earth and old leaves. Often in his dreams he heard the music of the forest—the drums, the tiny flutes, the excited whisper of the leaves.

It was harvest time now. The leaves on the trees were bright with gold and crimson. They were beginning to fall slowly with a whispering sound, like huge bright snowflakes. When a wind came they danced wildly for a minute before settling on the ground.

The farm was loaded with a hundred kinds of treasure now. Ears of corn hung heavily from withered stalks. Pumpkins were scattered like golden balls among the colorless cornstalks. There were apples on the trees, and potatoes and cabbages in the garden.

During these autumn days Aunt Patsey searched through the woods and fields for her winter supply of herbs. They would be used for stomachache, colds, toothache, and other illnesses. Sammy would go with her. He learned the names of many plants and where to look for them in the woods.

75

Another nice thing about autumn was the work parties. Neighbors would get together and help each other with their work. They would bring big dinners and everyone had a lot of fun.

There were apple-paring parties. There were corn shuckings. After the work was all done, the fiddlers got out their fiddles and the people would sing and dance.

Even when there were no parties, the evenings on the farm were pleasant. The fire roared high in the fireplace, and all the family would gather about the cheerful glow.

Uncle John would smoke his pipe and Aunt Patsey would spin. The children ate apples, cracked nuts, and drank cider.

Even the old dog, Shep, and the lazy cat, stretched out by the warm fireplace, enjoyed the autumn evenings.

"It will be time for the nut harvest soon," said Uncle John one frosty morning.

"Today!" the children chorused eagerly.

The nuts were thick under the trees—big walnuts with their thick, spicy hulls, and white hickory nuts whose shells fell away so easily. There were clusters of little shaggy hazelnuts, three-cornered beechnuts, and long, rich-flavored butternuts.

Besides the nuts which were good to eat, there were buckeyes, too. They were beautiful to look at, but they were deadly poison. Sammy knew better than to taste a buckeye, but he always gathered some because they were good for charms. Aunt Hanna knew the proper words to say over buckeyes which would turn them into magic.

When the nut harvest was over, then summer was really over—even Indian summer. After nut harvest the leaves fell and winds moaned coldly. Everything became brown-colored.

Nut harvest lasted all day, and Aunt Patsey

packed a large basket of bread and meat and apples. There was cider and milk to drink. Still at the end of the day the children were as hungry as wolves.

How good the house looked to them when it came in sight. The wood smoke curling from the chimney had a sweet smell. But the wonderful smell of supper cooking in the kitchen was best of all. Sammy began to sniff like old Shep, and to make a song:

"String beans, butter beans,
     Corn pone, biscuits, batter bread!
   Apple pie, peach pie, pumpkin pie and
        dumplings——"

Sammy stopped suddenly. There by the fireplace stood his mother. And there, waiting to surprise him, were all his family—Father, Orion, Pamela, Benjamin, and Henry!

"We've come to take you home!" cried Henry.

Sammy hugged his mother tightly. "I've got a present for you," he whispered. "It's something dandy. It's a big, shiny buckeye charm. It'll protect you from witches, goblins, ghosts, the evil eye, and nearly everything!"

Mrs. Clemens smiled and kissed him warmly.

The summer at Uncle John's house had been filled with happiness for Sammy. He would never forget it. He would come back next year.

Home Again

WHEN SAMMY woke up, he didn't know where he was. He looked about for his cousins, but he didn't see them. He looked twice at the little boy snuggled beside him in the low trundle bed before he remembered that he was home again. The boy beside him was his brother Henry.

Jennie was in the kitchen busily cooking. He hugged her joyfully. She told him how much he had grown and how she had missed him.

"I brought you a charm," said Sammy, handing her a satin-smooth buckeye. "It's magic, Jennie. Aunt Hanna said magic words over it."

Jennie was very glad to receive the charm.

She gave Sammy hot corn pone for his breakfast, with thick, dark cherry preserves.

Sammy could hardly wait to go outside to see if the Mississippi River was still as big, as wonderful, and as exciting as before.

"It is!" he whispered. "It's even bigger and grander than I remembered!"

He heard the hoarse blast of a steamboat whistle. The sound made a thrill go through him. He stood watching as the proud boat came up-river. He admired the thick smoke rising from the smokestacks. He wondered what it would be like to ride in such a palace.

"When I grow up I'm going to be a steamboat man," he said aloud. "I'd rather be a steamboat man than a king!"

Sammy didn't know how to describe the feeling that came over him when he looked at the great river. He only knew that he was glad to be home again, close to the river he loved.

Sammy sometimes watched his mother as she sewed quilt blocks together. He often wondered why she always put some dark blocks in with the bright-colored blocks.

"You need both light blocks and dark ones," his mother told him. "The dark blocks make the bright ones show up better."

"Days are like that, too," Sammy thought. Most of them were bright with happiness, but sometimes dark days came.

When Sammy was nine years old it seemed as if hard times made an extra number of dark blocks in the lives of the Clemens family.

The hard times started when Mr. Clemens tried to help one of his friends who had borrowed a great deal of money. His friend gave a note for the money. Sammy's father had signed his name to the note which meant that he would pay the money back if his friend could not.

These were days when many people were having a hard time getting money. Mr. Clemens' friend could not pay the note.

John Clemens had to sell everything to get enough money to pay the note. He sold his store, his house, his furniture, and even Jennie.

Parting with Jennie was the hardest thing of all. Everybody cried and Jennie cried.

The Clemens family did not sit around and cry about their hard times. Everybody tried to help. Father worked hard on his law practice and got a little office downtown.

The family rented another house and Mrs. Clemens took in boarders. Orion went to St. Louis where he got a job as a printer. He sent money home. Pamela gave music lessons.

Things looked brighter for a while. Suddenly Benjamin became very sick and died. There was great sadness in the family. Father looked more unsmiling than ever. Even Mother did not laugh quite so much. Hard work helped them to get over their sadness, and soon their bad luck began to leave them. They had better times.

"We will build a new house," Father planned. "There is a good place on Hill Street."

"Will it have an upstairs?" asked Pamela. Mr. Clemens indicated that it would.

Sammy was excited about the new house. He couldn't remember ever living in a brand new house before. This would not be just a log house. It would be a house of bright boards, and there would be an upstairs, too.

"I like the smell of new boards," thought Sammy. "I like the sound of hammering and building. Best of all, I can see the river even better from the new house!"

Being closer to the river brought its own temptations. From his front yard Sammy could get a good view of the packet boats going grandly up and down. It was torture—nothing short of torture, to see those boats, hear the splashing of their water wheels, listen to the alluring sound of their whistles. Sammy longed more than ever to be on board one of them.

Nobody seemed to understand the longing Sammy felt whenever he saw the packet boats.

"You're not even ten yet," Orion would say. "You can't expect to have all your wishes now. You have to wait and be patient!"

Pamela was likely to give him a loving hug and laugh at his longings.

"I'm glad you're just my little brother and not a big old steamboat captain," she said. "Don't wish your life away, honey. You've got years of traveling yet!"

"Who's sure of that?" returned Sammy darkly. "I might die of the measles or from eating green apples or getting gored by a bull. I might even get shot down in the street!"

Pamela laughed more than ever.

"Nothing like that will happen to you!" she declared. "You've got nine lives—like Old Peter."

Old Peter was the only remaining one of the kittens that had traveled in the willow basket from Florida. Paul, Simon, Moses, and Methuselah had gone the way of all good cats. Goldie now seemed as old as old Aunt Hanna, dreaming out her days in the sunshine.

Little Peter, skinniest of the kittens, had become Old Peter, a big, tough fighting tomcat. Old Peter had been chased by dogs and cows. He had had many battles with other cats. He had lost an ear to a furious rat and part of his tail when a wagon ran over it. But he lived through every danger and enjoyed every minute.

Old Peter loved Sammy and often followed him on long walks through the woods and along the banks of Bear Creek. He brought Sammy gifts, too—gifts which seemed valuable to a cat.

He brought Sammy gifts of mice and moles, rabbits and chipmunks. As a rule, Peter ate his own gifts when his master refused them. It was Peter who gave Sammy a pet frog which went with him on a thrilling adventure.

One fine October day Sammy and Peter had gone for a walk in the meadow. They came across a small spotted frog. It was a leopard frog on his way to a winter home in the marsh.

Sammy thought a leopard frog would make a nice pet and reached for the small creature. But the frog was too quick for him and got away. In a minute he was out of sight.

"Oh, pshaw!" said Sammy disappointed. "I wasn't going to hurt you."

A few minutes later Sammy stopped to look at a red admiral butterfly on a gentian stalk. He heard an ear-splitting screech. Here came Old Peter carrying the small leopard frog carefully in his jaws.

Sammy took the peeper. He was amazed that such a loud noise could come from so small a creature. The leopard frog swelled out his under jaw like a balloon, squeaked angrily, and struggled to get away.

Sammy held on. "I'll bet you could even learn to sing," he said admiringly. "I bet you could learn to jump higher than any frog in the state of Missouri. Your name shall be Ike and you're my champion pet frog."

Ike got over his wild ways and became a good pet for Sammy. He lived in an old sauerkraut jar, where he could jump and splash.

Ike seemed to enjoy his life. He ate the bugs, flies, bread crumbs, and other foods which Sammy brought him, but he was always trying to get out of the jar.

Sammy kept an old rag tied over the top of the jar for Ike's legs grew longer and stronger with each jump.

With a piece of thick, soft string tied to one of Ike's legs, Sammy would take the frog for a walk. Ike jumped high, thinking he was free.

One day when they were out walking together, the packetboat came majestically around the curve in the river and docked at Hannibal.

"I can't stand it!" whispered Sammy, looking at the floating heaven there before him. "I can't wait till I'm old. I can't!"

The boat seemed to be waiting just for him, calling out to him. Without really stopping to think Sammy pulled in Ike's leash, dropped the frog into his pocket, and rushed to the river.

Sammy was lucky. Nobody seemed to notice him as he slipped up the gangplank and onto the upper deck. He crept under one of the lifeboats on the deck and waited, getting his breath. He was on a steamboat at last!

"We made it, Ike," he whispered, taking the frog from his pocket. "We got our wish!"

Ike only goggled with his big eyes. He had not yet got his greatest wish.

At last a bell rang. The wheel began to turn. Sammy was riding a steamboat! This was the most glorious day of his life. He crawled out from his hiding place so he could watch the scenery along the shore.

A terrific crash of thunder made Sammy jump. A minute later it began to rain. At first the shower felt pleasant, but it turned into a torrent that threatened to wash him off deck.

He heard the shouts of passengers as they ran from their cabins and the sound of crew members on deck. Quickly he crawled back under the lifeboat. But he did not crawl far enough or fast enough. His legs were sticking out.

"What's this?" he heard someone say. The next minute a strong arm jerked him out. "A stowaway, eh? And what's that you're hiding in your pocket?"

"That's Ike," Sammy replied. "He's a frog. He's a high jumper. He's my pet." He removed Ike from his pocket and pulled off the leash to show his pet proudly.

This was just the chance Ike had been waiting for. In one great leap he rose high out of Sammy's hand, sailed out over the rail, and swelled his throat in a loud cry of triumph. He was indeed a high jumper. He had been practicing for this jump a long time.

"He got away! Ike got away!" Sammy cried. He hardly knew whether to cry or to be proud of Ike's success.

A deck hand saw Sammy's tears. "Never mind, lad," said the man. "He'll be all right. Frogs are right at home in the water."

The deck hand's voice became suddenly stern. "You come on down to the captain's cabin now and explain yourself."

Sammy wondered how to explain the longing that had pulled him so. But what was there to explain? He had wanted to go on a steamboat and he went on a steamboat! It was that simple.

The captain put Sammy ashore at the town of Louisiana where some of Mrs. Clemens' cousins lived. They took the runaway safely back home.

Sammy paid for his great experience with a good thrashing. But when the pain of the punishment wore off, Sammy looked back on the trip with pleasure. It was funny how things became more exciting when they were over.

Sammy was only sorry that the rainstorm had ruined his plans and kept him from making a longer trip. But nothing could change the glorious fact that he had taken a trip on a steamboat! His greatest wish had come true!

Ike had made a wish come true, too. For a long time he had tried to get away. He wanted to be free. He never gave up trying and he got his big wish the same day that Sammy got his.

The New Neighbor

THE CLEMENS' new house was now finished, and the family was getting settled. Sammy was so excited he hardly knew what he was doing.

"You're just like a chicken with its head off!" said his mother when Sammy bumped into the tray of dishes she was carrying. "Why don't you go outdoors for a while?"

Sammy went outside. He climbed a tree in the front yard. He sat there looking around and feeling like a king on a throne.

He looked at the house across the street. While he watched, the door of the house opened and a little girl came out. She was rather a pretty girl, with a ruffled pinafore and long black curls.

When she saw towheaded Sammy perched up in the tree she began to laugh. "You look just like a little ugly baby robin with your red hair," she called to him.

"You look like an old black crow with your long black hair," Sammy retorted. "You sound like an old crow, too, when you laugh."

The crow was really Sammy's favorite bird, with its glistening smooth feathers, strong graceful wings, and jolly manner.

"Baby robins are the ugliest birds in the world," the girl called, as she came closer to her front fence. She looked sharply at Sammy.

Sammy sat up and swung a little on the tree limb, deep in thought.

"I know a charm against witches," he said. "I know some good ghost stories, too. I know a place where goblins come out and have dances.

My Uncle John has a slave woman that used to take care of Moses when he was a baby!"

"I don't believe any of those things," the little girl replied, "but come on down anyway. I've got a sack with seven peppermint balls in it. You can have one."

"My name's Sammy Clemens," he said when he reached the ground. "What's yours?"

"Mine's Laura Hawkins," she replied, holding out the striped paper sack. "Here, take one."

"Let's go down and look at the river," said Sammy. "I'm going to be a steamboat pilot when I grow up. What are you going to be?"

"A schoolteacher," answered Laura. "Or maybe a preacher's wife or a missionary."

"I'd like to be a clown in the circus, too," said Sammy. He was thinking of the showboats which sometimes came up the river. "Maybe I'll be a clown part of the time and a steamboat pilot the rest of the time."

The children walked down the street together. Laura pointed to a tumble-down-looking shack near the river's edge.

"A drunkard lives in that house," she told Sammy. "His name is Old Man Blankenship. He's got a boy named Tom."

"It's not much of a house," remarked Sammy.

"Old Man Blankenship is as mean as can be," Laura went on. "He's even mean to his own boy. He whips Tom, too. He's dirty and ugly and mean as an old river rat."

Sammy was interested. He wondered what it would be like to have such a father. He didn't know then that some day Old Man Blankenship's son would be one of his best friends.

SUNDAY PRESENT

"Why do Sundays have to be the prettiest days?" wondered Sammy, as his mother scrubbed and scoured his ears. "It wouldn't be so bad having to go to Sunday school and church if the weather was ugly!"

Today the weather was beautiful. The sun was shining, but not too much. There was a soft breeze that seemed to whisper, "Come!"

There would be flowers blooming in the woods, Sammy knew. Birds would be making nests, and he could watch them. He might find a rabbit's nest buried deep in the ground. It might even be filled with soft baby rabbits.

Sammy tried and tried to think of a good reason for staying away from Sunday school, but Mrs. Clemens would not listen. She just scoured harder than ever.

When they reached the church Mrs. Clemens looked around, but she did not see Sammy.

"Sammy forgot his Sunday school penny, Mother," Henry whispered to Mrs. Clemens. "He had to go back after it."

Sammy really had forgotten his penny. He did not like to be without a present for the collection bag when it came past him. He ran back home very fast through the sunlight.

It took Sammy a good while to find the penny. He was tired when he started to church again—too tired to run. His steps became slower.

"Mother will be ashamed if I come in late," Sammy thought. "It makes her angry to hear a noise during prayer."

The more he thought about it the more it seemed to Sammy that he shouldn't go into the church late. He came to the turn in the street. After a minute or so he took the turn which led to the woods.

Sammy spent the lovely morning wandering about the woods in the sunshine. He caught a little green garter snake, only a few inches long. It was a wonderful thrill to Sammy because he had always wanted a live snake.

"Maybe this snake will grow into a monster," he thought. "Then I can have a show with it. It will be a river show. I'll even let Laura be in the show, too."

Suddenly Sammy was very hungry. He noticed that the sun was almost directly above him. He was afraid his mother would not like the way he looked. His arms and legs were scratched with briars, and his face was dirty. There were torn places in his clean shirt.

Sammy had really meant to go back to the

church. He really hadn't intended to forget his penny. Now he discovered that he had lost his penny and church was over.

"There's only one thing left to do, and that's to give the snake to Mother," he thought mournfully. He hated to give up the snake, but he had to do something to pay up.

When he reached home, Sammy presented the snake to his mother, but she did not want it. She threw it outdoors and it wriggled away quickly through the grass.

That night Sammy had to go to church after all. He had to sit with his father and mother while Henry slept peacefully at home.

Sammy looked so sad all the while he was in church that Mrs. Clemens felt sure he was sorry for his naughty actions. But Sammy wasn't thinking about his punishment. He was thinking about his little lost snake and all the plans which had been lost with it.

The Club

MR. TRUMBULL, the bookstore keeper, had a great stack of brightly covered books about the famous and wicked river pirate John Murrell. Sammy was on his way to the bookstore to buy one of these books which cost ten cents each. Ten cents was a lot of money to Sammy.

From cover to cover the books were filled with thrilling stories about the wicked pirate and his gang of river robbers.

Sammy liked to read the books about John Murrell, but his mother thought they were not good reading for young boys. So Sammy was always very careful to hide his books in a safe place—a place where he thought his mother would not be able to find them.

He stopped at the town pump to get a drink. When he raised his head, a strange boy was looking at him. The boy was about Sammy's age or maybe a couple of years older. He looked like a tramp with his torn clothes, dirty face, and shaggy hair. He gave Sammy a friendly grin.

"Who are you?" the boy asked Sammy.

Sammy gave his name.

"I'm Tom Blankenship," the boy replied. "I live down by the river."

Sammy was very interested. So this was Old Man Blankenship's son. He was almost a tramp. He didn't go to school, or wash and dress up like other boys, or eat meals at regular times, or anything like that.

Sammy opened his hand and showed the money he was holding. "I'm going to buy a book," he said. "It's about Murrell, the river pirate. It's a very exciting story. Would you like to read it, Tom?" he offered.

"I never had time to learn reading," answered Tom, "but I can smoke a pipe. I bet you can't do that."

Sammy shook his head. "No, I can't," he said.

"How'd you like to read to me?" asked Tom. "We'll go out behind my house where nobody will bother us."

Sammy went into the store and spent his money for the most exciting story about John Murrell that he could find. The boys walked together to the shack where Tom lived.

"My dad's gone," said Tom, "so you don't need to be afraid." He got a box for Sammy to sit on.

A long time passed pleasantly while Sammy read to Tom. Sammy was glad he met Tom.

"There's a cave down the river a-ways from here," Tom said. "We could use that for our club if we had one."

"Let's get up a club!" cried Sammy. He was always quick to take up an exciting idea.

"I know some boys that could be in the club," he went on. "They're not very dangerous and they can't smoke, but they'll do. They're the Bowen boys and Will Pitts and John Briggs—"

"I can cook over an outdoor fire," interrupted Tom. "And I know how to get to Glasscock's Island. It's haunted you know!"

"My!" said Sammy admiringly. He had never had a friend like Tom Blakenship. He could hardly wait to get the club started.

Mrs. Clemens scolded Sammy when he went home. It was long past dinnertime. She was afraid he had fallen in the river again.

"I've got something else to do besides fall in the river," said Sammy proudly.

What fun it was going to be to explore the cave and the island, to cook meals outdoors, and to learn to smoke! A club of boys could even build a raft and take trips on the river, too. A great many ideas for fun suddenly popped into Sammy's head.

"I've got a lot of exciting things to do, Mother!" he exclaimed.

THE CAVE

Six boys walked along the dusty road which led from Hannibal to McDowell's cave. The cave was about two miles south of town.

The boys carried bundles of different kinds. Some of them had food. One carried a rusty frying pan and a great coffeepot. Another boy had a package of bright-covered books. The others were carrying blankets.

Sammy and the club were going to have a picnic in the cave. They were going to build a fire and cook roasting ears, bacon, and coffee.

Sammy would read to the boys from the paperbacked books exciting stories about Murrell the river pirate, Captain Kidd the ocean pirate, Robin Hood of the forest, and Daniel Boone the wilderness scout.

People passing the boys on the road thought that they were six plain, harmless youngsters. That was the way they looked, but to themselves they were a fierce, dangerous gang of river pirates—pirates who were going to a cave to count their treasure and make plans.

They finally came to the hill where there was a doorway into the cave. It was arched like the capital letter A.

Sammy stood before the doorway and said in a fierce tone, "Give the secret password!"

"Black magic," said each boy, as fiercely as he could. One by one the boys entered the cool dimness of the cave.

"Today we're going to explore for buried treasure," said Sammy.

The cave spread through the hill like a huge goblin's castle. Nobody had ever explored all its halls and passages. There were long tunnels in it, deep pools, strange piles of rock, and queer-looking things like icicles that hung down from the ceiling.

"I'd rather count the treasure we've already got," said Will Pitts, who was a little bit afraid to go far back in the cave.

The Bowen boys wanted to work on their disguises. Their disguises were what made them look different and dangerous. They had long beards, curly mustaches which hung over their mouths, and masks which would have scared even pirate Murrell.

Sammy had a special charm to help them find the treasure. It was a black magic charm. A slave down at the dock had given it to him.

"You build a fire," said the dock hand, "throw this magic charm into the middle of it and say

'Black Magic' three times. Then you'll get a sign that tells you where to look for the treasure!"

Excitedly the boys built the fire and held their breaths while Sammy got ready to throw the magic charm into the flame. Of course none of them knew the charm was just a bullet which the slave had picked up somewhere.

"Black Magic! Black Magic! Black Magic!" cried Sammy, tossing the charm into the fire.

There was a loud noise, a flash, and a cloud of smoke which scared the boys nearly to death. Then the next minute another cloud rose up angrily from the side of the cave.

"The sign!" cried Sammy eagerly.

"Bats!" said Will Pitts in a disgusted voice. "Just plain old bats!"

The queer little winged animals which lived in the cave had been disturbed from their sleep. They flew about squeaking and fluttering.

"Bats are not treasure," said John Briggs. He

had fully expected to see a chest of gold fly open at his feet.

"Bats aren't good for anything," said one of the Bowen boys.

"You can't even eat bats," his brother echoed. "Even a cat won't eat them."

"It's a sign, all the same," Sammy declared. He was not discouraged.

"Just you wait," he went on. "I bet some time you'll find out that bats are regular treasures. I just know they're useful for something. Didn't the magic charm tell us so?"

Cross Mr. Cross

SAMMY'S THOUGHTS kept slipping out the dusty, buzzing schoolroom and flying back to Uncle John's farm. He just couldn't keep his mind on sums or geography or the proper way to hold a goose-quill pen.

The days were getting hot now. Wasps buzzed angrily about the room. Honeybees, always so industrious, strayed in now and then.

"I bet they don't like the smell of the chalk and the dust and the books either," thought Sammy as he watched the bees.

He thought of all the beehives in the back-yard of Uncle John's big log house. The peach and apple trees would be covered with bloom now. The bees would be having a good time.

Uncle John's slaves would be busy, too, with the spring crops. The great woods behind their cabins would be coming to life.

"Samuel Clemens," the schoolmaster's harsh voice interrupted Sammy's daydreaming. "Give the multiplication table of nine."

"Nine times one is nine," said Sammy. He was sure of that much, but for the life of him he couldn't think of the rest of the table.

The teacher's name was Mr. Cross. He was a severe teacher who really used the switches which he cut from the beech tree in front of the schoolhouse.

It made Mr. Cross very angry for his pupils to dawdle or fail to know their lessons. He gave Sammy a good lick across the shoulders with one of his switches and called on someone else for the table of nine.

"Why are teachers always so cross?" Sammy wondered. He looked wistfully through the dusty window. He began to smile.

"Why is Mr. Cross so cross?" he said to himself. The more he thought about it, the funnier it seemed that Mr. Cross should have a name that fitted him so well.

The schoolteacher glared around the room ready to switch anybody who was not working. Everybody seemed busy. Even Sammy Clemens seemed to be working hard at his lesson.

"That idler smiles too much," thought Mr. Cross to himself. "He is even smiling to himself while he does his lesson. That shows he will never amount to anything in this world. Lessons should be taken seriously."

The teacher was about to go over and see what lesson Sammy was working on and perhaps find some fault in it. Just then a little girl asked him to sharpen her goose-quill pen.

114

Presently the schoolteacher noticed that something seemed to be very funny. The children were giggling to themselves or smiling. Only Sammy Clemens looked very serious as he studied his arithmetic lesson.

Mr. Cross rushed back and seized a slate from one of the girls. There was something written on it. When Mr. Cross read the lines, he looked more angry than ever.

> "Cross by name,
> Cross by nature.
> Cross jumped over
> A rotten potater!"

"Who wrote this?" thundered Mr. Cross. Nobody answered. All the children looked at him with their eyes wide and innocent. They were trying hard not to laugh.

Mr. Cross wanted to whip the poet who had written the rhyme about him, but since he was

written the rhyme about him, but since he was not quite sure who it was, he had to put off the whipping.

PIPE DREAMS

Sammy had often heard Uncle John and other people talk about pipe dreams. Uncle John used to sit by the hour quietly smoking with a far-away look in his eyes.

"I'm just having pipe dreams," he would say, if anybody asked him what he was thinking.

Sammy thought it would be nice to have some pipe dreams of his own. That was one reason why he wanted Tom to teach him to smoke.

"This is a good day to learn to smoke," thought Sammy one bright pleasant morning. He went past Tom's house. As usual Tom was not doing much of anything.

"Will you teach me to smoke?" asked Sammy. "I've got four pork sandwiches and some dried-

116

apple pie and two pickles in this sack. Let's go some place and eat and smoke."

"Sure," agreed Tom, who was always ready for anything. "I've been thinking it was about time for you to learn."

"We'd better go some place where nobody will be watching," said Sammy. "How about down by Bear Creek?"

"Sure," agreed Tom again. "Bear Creek's a fine place. It's shady down there under the willow trees. Nobody will be looking for us."

They took along fishing poles and string so they could fish while they smoked. Tom believed in saving all the work he could. He fastened the poles so that the strings would hang in the water and catch the fish all by themselves.

Sammy felt excited and rather wicked. Tom got out his old black pipe and his bag of strong coarse tobacco.

"Did you ever hear about any bears down

here?" Sammy asked while Tom filled the pipe bowl with tobacco leaves.

"All the bears down here got killed off a long time ago," answered Tom as he worked to get the pipe lighted. "Of course, there's ghost bears and goblin bears though. They stay close around the place where they used to live before they got killed."

"You never did see any of them, did you?" asked Sammy.

A little puff of pale, strong-smelling smoke began to rise from the pipe. Tom took several strong pulls before he answered.

"Sure, lots of times," said Tom. "Most any night you can see them walking up and down the bank and over the water. Some folks say they're only river mist, but those are folks that have poor eyesight."

For the next several minutes the boys forgot about everything except the smoking lesson.

118

The smoke was very strong. Sammy choked and strangled and tears ran down his cheeks. He wondered how anybody ever managed to smoke a pipe in an easy, careless way.

"This is almost as bad as pain-killer!" Sammy gasped, but he kept on. Soon he stopped choking and coughing, but the strong fumes went to his head. He began to feel very strange. His head felt light and strange.

Presently he thought that he saw something white move slowly across the water below him. He looked more closely. Yes, it certainly seemed to be a bear—a strange, furry, white bear which moved along in a slow, ghostly way.

"Do you see anything?" Sammy whispered.

"Nothing much," Tom answered cheerfully. "Just water and trees and things like that. Do you s'pose it's time to eat, Sam?"

Sammy took a big gulp of pipe smoke and looked down the creek. Yes, he was almost sure he saw two bears now—at least two bears, and perhaps three or four. It was a little hard for him to see, but there must be anyway four or five bears. And they were walking across the water, of all things!

"What's the matter?" asked Tom, when he heard Sammy moan.

"I'm terrible sick," answered Sammy. "Oh, Tom, I think I'm going to die. I'm almost sure I'm going to die!"

Now Sammy remembered that Jennie had often told him that ghosts came to people who were going to die. Animal ghosts were the worst kind. And there was a whole flock of them down there, just waiting for him to die. Sammy felt sick enough to die, too. He couldn't ever remember feeling quite this sick before.

After a while Sammy took a long nap. When he wakened he felt a little better, but he didn't care to smoke any more.

That night Sammy dreamed about smoke-colored goblin bears walking the waters of Bear Creek. He moaned and threshed and made so much noise that his mother went into his room to see what was the matter.

"It's the bears, the goblin bears," he cried sleepily. Mrs. Clemens laughed.

"Wake up, Sammy," she called. "You're having nightmares. There are no goblins!"

Sammy sat up in bed and rubbed his eyes. He was glad to find himself at home with his mother near him.

"You're just having nightmares, Sammy," Mrs. Clemens said again.

"No, Mother, it's pipe dreams I'm having," replied Sammy. "And I don't like them a bit!"

Melons by Moonlight

ONE HOT NIGHT in late summer, Sammy awoke from his sleep. The moon was high and bright. It was shining through the window, making the room almost as light as day.

"How hot it is tonight!" thought Sammy. He felt thirsty and went downstairs to get a drink of water. The pump was on the back porch.

Peter, the cat, was walking about the yard in that proud, quiet way of cats.

"Don't you ever sleep at night, Peter?" said Sammy. "Or maybe you think that mice taste better at night than in the daytime."

The water didn't seem very cool. Sammy kept

123

thinking about melons—great big juicy water-melons. He loved watermelons. There was nothing so delicious on a hot day as the pink, sweet inside of a ripe watermelon.

Sammy looked around. A heavy dew lay like a silver veil on everything. He could see Mr. McDaniel's melon patch from where he stood.

"I bet those melons would be good and cool tonight," he thought to himself.

His Uncle John used to put melons in the spring where he would leave them for several hours. This seemed to make the melons juicier than ever—sweeter and more crisp, too.

"Um-m-m-m!" murmured Sammy. "I wish I could be down by the spring house now, break-ing open a big melon and eating the heart of it!"

Uncle John's spring house, however, was more than thirty miles away. But, there was a melon patch full of melons not a mile away.

"I believe I'll take a little walk," whispered

Sammy. He slipped back into the house and pulled on an old pair of trousers. Then, softly as Peter, he came outside again. He went down to Tom's house.

In a few minutes, two figures appeared in the moonlight. It hadn't been hard to waken Tom. He was always ready for anything.

"Let's wake up the rest of the gang," said Sammy. "They'd feel better if they had a good walk in the moonlight."

The windows were open in most of the houses, so Tom and Sammy didn't have much trouble getting the gang together.

"Where are we going to walk?" yawned Will Pitts. He hadn't really wanted to get up just to take a walk, but it was a rule of the club to do what the leader said.

"We're going to Mr. McDaniel's melon patch," replied Sammy. "His melons need to be thinned out. If some of the melons are picked, the ones that are left will get bigger and redder and sweeter."

"That's right," agreed John Briggs. "My father picks off baskets of green peaches each summer, because if too many are left on the tree they'll all be little and sour."

"The little ones would have a better chance," said Tom wisely, "if your father would pick off the big ones."

All this time the boys were walking down the quiet, moonlit street toward Mr. McDaniel's melon patch near the river.

"Do you suppose Mr. McDaniel will want us to get into his melon patch?" asked Will in a worried voice. "He's kind of a cross man."

"He's cross because he's so busy," answered Sammy. "He's one of the busiest men in Hannibal. He's too busy to think about melons."

"We'll be doing him a good deed," said Tom. "We won't charge him anything."

"We'll eat only what we pick," said Sammy.

"How many should we thin out?" asked one of the Bowen boys, looking over the patch.

"Not more than we can eat by ourselves," replied Sammy. "About six apiece, I reckon."

However, six melons each were more than the boys could carry. John Briggs and the Bowen boys took two melons each, and Will Pitts stopped with one big one. Sammy and Tom each took three melons.

"We've done a kind act for Mr. McDaniel," said Sammy breathlessly, as the boys carried their melons out of the patch. "The rest of his melons will grow better now."

The boys found a place where they could throw the rinds into the river, as soon as they had scooped out and eaten the pink pulp.

When Sammy went home at last he wasn't thirsty any more. He didn't feel hungry either.

"Nothing in the world is so good as a ripe

watermelon eaten in the moonlight," he thought as he crawled back into bed. "But I wouldn't want any more now!"

The next day Sammy did not feel very well and he had no appetite for his meals. Mrs. Clemens was a little worried.

"Go outdoors a while," she said. "You'll feel more like eating if you have some exercise. You can pull weeds from the garden."

Sammy didn't feel like pulling weeds, but he went outside anyway. In the afternoon Henry came running to call him.

"Uncle John's here, Sammy!" said Henry. "He's brought us something. It's something you just love! Hurry!"

"What is it?" asked Sammy disinterestedly.

"It's watermelon," Henry went on eagerly.

"Who said I like watermelons?" cried Sammy angrily. "And why do you talk so much? I don't see why you make me eat them."

He went into the house and looked at the big pieces of pink and green melon on the table. Some people thought whippings were pretty bad, but right now Sammy wasn't so sure.

"Whippings aren't so bad," thought he, holding his stomach.

Right now poor Sammy would willingly take a whipping in exchange for such a stomachache.

A USE FOR BATS

One hot night the Clemens family was awakened by loud screams. Sammy and Henry sat up in bed and looked at each other with frightened eyes.

"Do you suppose anybody's getting killed?" whispered Henry.

"Those screams are coming from Pamela's room," said Sammy. "Likely she's just had a nightmare. Or maybe she's walking in her sleep and stepped on a tack."

"You're the only one in this family who walks in his sleep," replied Henry.

Sammy didn't like to be reminded of his sleep-walking. He was about to throw a pillow at his brother when more screams interrupted him.

"It might be a runaway slave!" said Sammy hopefully. "Or maybe Pamela saw a ghost!"

"It's in my hair!" screamed Pamela. "There's two of them! They're after me!"

Suddenly Sammy remembered something. "It's my bats!" he said to Henry. "I suppose they've got out of their box." He raced down the hall to his sister's room.

Earlier in the day Sammy had caught four bats in the cave and put them in a box. He brought them home thinking they might be tamed for pets. He had placed the box in Pamela's room because it was shady there.

130

Sammy could never understand why he was the only one in the family who liked bats. He thought they were such interesting creatures with their big, funny wings, their little sharp faces, and their squeaking voices.

When he reached Pamela's room his mother and father were there with lighted candles. Pamela was jumping about the room in fright. The bats were flying about her head.

Mr. and Mrs. Clemens were quite angry with Sammy. Mrs. Clemens was especially angry.

Two of the bats got away, but Mr. Clemens killed the other two with the broom.

"A good thing, too," said Henry. "Bats aren't good for anything except witches' charms."

"Bats make good pets," declared Sammy, who loved all animals. "Bats can fly, too, most animals can only walk. Besides, if you were lost in a cave and didn't have anything to eat, you could live on bats for days and days."

"Bats are no use in the world," Henry repeated stubbornly.

One day, not long after this incident, Sammy and his gang went down to the cave. Some men were loading something onto wagons. At first the boys thought it might be buried treasure. When they got closer, they saw it was only great heaps of trash, bat droppings, and dead bats which had piled up in the cave.

The boys were worried that the men would drive them out of their play place.

"These droppings are called guano," the men explained. "There's saltpeter in guano. Saltpeter can be used to make gunpowder. Gunpowder is going to help us win the war."

The year was now 1846 and the United States was at war with Mexico.

"You mean you make gunpowder out of bats?" Sammy's eyes got very big and bright.

"Well, it's something like that," laughed one

of the men. "You never thought bats could be so useful, did you? Never dreamed that a little old bat could fight a war, did you?"

Sammy was pleased—just as pleased as he had been the day Orion got his job on the St. Louis newspaper. Just as pleased as the time Pamela won first prize at school.

"I knew all the time that bats were good for something," Sammy replied happily.

Pirate's Island

AT SUNRISE one Saturday morning in summer, Sammy and the club pushed their raft into the water. The boys were on their way to Glasscock's Island. They were going to spend a day doing the things they liked best—swimming, digging for treasure, and planning the adventures of their pirate gang.

The boys had brought along a basket of bread and meat, salt, potatoes, roasting ears, and corn meal. They had also brought fishing lines, knives, and a shovel.

"No matter what happens," they vowed, "we'll be ready for it."

"Did you bring the book?" one of the boys asked Sammy.

Sammy nodded his head.

The book was a paperbacked book with a bright cover which showed the wicked John Murrell robbing a boat. It was a very exciting book all about the adventures of that wicked pirate.

The boys had to keep the book hidden and read it only when their parents could not see them. Most of their parents did not like for them to read about such a wicked man.

"I wonder how many boats John Murrell and his gang have robbed in their lives?" said Will Pitts, as they floated along the river.

"Hundreds of 'em, I guess," answered Sammy. "Maybe even thousands. He's got a big gang— over twenty-five hundred men."

The boys could hardly imagine so many pirates in one gang.

"I wonder where he hides all the time," said Tom. "I'd like to see what he looks like!"

"I'd like to see his treasure," said Sammy. "I wonder where he keeps it."

"I wouldn't be surprised if a lot of it was right around Hannibal," said Tom. "The cave would be a good place to hide treasure. Nobody could ever find it there!"

The boys thought of other places where the pirate might have hidden stolen treasure.

"Pirates always like islands," said Will. He had been reading about Captain Kidd.

"Our island would be one of the finest places for a bandit crew," Sammy told his friends. "I wouldn't be surprised if there was a thousand dollars' worth of gold buried on it—or even six or ten thousand dollars' worth!"

"It would be a great day in Hannibal if we could come home with five or six thousand dollars' worth of gold," said Will.

"Likely there would be a parade," planned Sammy with his quick imagination. "It'd be a lot bigger than most parades. Course, we'd all be at the head of it!"

Planning their wealth and what they would do with it made the boys' trip to the island seem short. The island was covered with thick, wiry grass, willows, and wild plum trees. There was a lot of scrubby underbrush, too.

The boys could hide there and not be seen. Yet they could see everything else—the broad water, the passing boats, the little town, drowsy against the hillside, and the deep green forest beyond the town.

The hours were lazy, yet they seemed to go too fast, because they were so filled with happiness and fun. Sometimes men in other boats would pass by and hail the boys.

Once that day, while the boys were digging at a place where they hoped to find treasure, they looked up to see a man watching them with a curious look. The stranger was very tall and broad-shouldered. He was wearing the bearskin cap and leather leggings of a riverman.

The boys thought the stranger was probably a tramp or an old flatboat man. He carried a rifle and he was chewing tobacco. There was a tall, black bottle sticking out of his pocket.

When Sammy told him they were digging for pirate treasure, the man laughed and laughed.

"You'd better be careful that old John Murrell doesn't see you," the man replied. "If he does he might be doing some more burying, and it wouldn't be gold either!" He winked at them and walked away.

After he had gone a strange, exciting idea came to Sammy. Suppose he had been the pirate Murrell himself. The more he thought about it, the more Sammy was sure the man was the famous pirate. He soon convinced the others.

"We must never tell anybody about this!" Sammy said, as he and the boys headed home. "Especially our mothers. It would worry them to death to know that Pirate Murrell had almost captured and killed us!"

The boys shivered. They didn't know whether to be afraid because of their narrow escape, or whether to be proud because they had actually seen the famous wicked pirate.

A day or so later Mrs. Clemens was reading the newspaper. She looked up from her reading in a rather relieved way.

"We won't be bothered by hearing about John Murrell any longer," she said to her husband.

Sammy listened intently. His heart was beating very fast. "Why not, Mother?" he asked.

"Because he's dead," his mother replied. "It's a good thing for this country, too. He'd been in prison. You see, Sammy, what happens to a wicked man who won't do what he should?"

"Are you sure he's dead, Mother?" asked Sammy, in a disappointed voice. "How long had he been in prison?"

"Of course he's dead," said Mrs. Clemens. "The paper wouldn't say so if he wasn't. And he was in prison a good while."

Sammy was disappointed. He hurried out to find Tom to tell him the bad news.

"It wasn't Murrell the pirate we saw on the island," Sammy told Tom. "He's dead. My mother saw the news in the paper."

Tom had another idea. "Then it was his ghost we saw!" he declared. "I thought all the time it was a ghost. Ghosts always come back."

Sammy did not doubt but what Tom was right. He had heard so much about ghosts and goblins, haunts and charms, that they were quite real to him.

It made Sammy a little scared to think that he had been so close to a ghost, especially the ghost of that wicked pirate John Murrell. At the same time, it made him feel important, too.

"I wish I'd known it was a ghost," Sammy said to Tom. "I would have liked to shake hands with him. I never did touch a ghost. I wonder what a ghost feels like!"

"I don't know as I really care," answered Tom, looking about in a scared way. "I never wanted to get too close to a ghost!"

Cub Printer

"DON'T CRY, Mother," said Sammy bravely. "We'll all help. I'll go to work!"

The year was 1847 and Sammy was now twelve years old. It was a sad year, too, for Mr. Clemens had died that year.

Mrs. Clemens wiped her tears and put her arms around her slender, flaxen-haired son.

"I hate for you to leave school," she said. "I'd always hoped you could go to college. I hoped you would be a lawyer like your father."

"I can get a job," said Sammy. "Mr. Ament, at the *Missouri Courier*, wants a boy to work in the printing office. He'll take me."

"I think it would be a good idea," said Orion. Orion had come back home from St. Louis to help the family make plans for the future.

"I am only twenty years old and I get ten dollars a week," he went on. "The printing trade is a good one for Sammy to learn."

The very next week Sammy went to work for Mr. Ament. It was April now, and the cold wet weather which had caused Mr. Clemens' illness was gone. The sun was shining brightly.

It was hard for Sammy to stay in the hot, dusty printing office on such a day. The outdoors seemed to be calling him. The river looked more beautiful than ever. Sammy longed to be outside, but he couldn't run away whenever he pleased now. Now he had to stick to his job.

His job was to do all sorts of errands around the shop. He had to learn how to run the printing press, too. He also had to set little letters into lines of type.

Mr. Ament did not pay Sammy in money. Instead he gave Sammy clothes and food.

"When you have learned the trade," said the editor, "you will get money for your work."

Sometimes Sammy got hungry between meals. He often went to the corner of the room to get a raw potato, or turnip, or even some cabbage to eat. There were usually several baskets of vegetables sitting about the office. Many of Mr. Ament's customers paid for the newspaper with vegetables or wood.

At three o'clock each day Sammy's work was done. Then he could go to the river and be with his friends, the rivermen, for a while.

NEWSPAPER TROUBLES

Fourteen-year-old Sammy was excited. As he went down the street he shouted to his friends, "Have you heard the news?"

Today as he walked into the dusty little newspaper office and got ready to work, Sammy felt differently about it.

"Soon this will be *our* newspaper," he murmured. "Then we can say what we please in it!"

Orion had decided to come back to Hannibal and buy the *Missouri Courier* from Mr. Ament. Sammy thought it would be much more interesting to work on his brother's newspaper than on Mr. Ament's paper.

Sammy had sometimes wanted to write things for the newspaper, but Mr. Ament had never liked any of the things he wrote.

"You're a printer's helper," the editor had said crossly, "not a poet. Stick to your work and don't waste time trying to write things nobody wants to read anyway!"

"When Orion is editor of this newspaper," Sammy had planned happily, "I'll be able to write poems whenever I want to."

146

There was another newspaper in Hannibal. There was always a race between the two papers to see which one could get the most subscribers.

"I plan to make the *Courier* the finest paper in this part of Missouri," said Orion.

"We must make it interesting so more people will subscribe to it," thought Sammy.

While he put lines of type together, Sammy tried to think of things that would be interesting for people to read.

"Everybody likes to read about love," he mused. "I will write a poem about love."

Sammy thought a long while. Then he wrote a poem about a young girl in town. The girl's name was Mary. Sammy admired Mary very much, so it was not hard for him to write a love poem to her. The title of the poem was, "To Mary in Hannibal."

When the type was set, Sammy discovered that the title of the poem was too long. He had to take out some of the letters. Thus when the poem was printed, it read:

"TO MARY IN H - - - L"

This made the title look like profane language, which was quite a shock to some of the people in Hannibal! Many of them stopped Orion on the street to tell him that he should not print profane words is his newspaper.

Orion was angry. He gave Sammy a good scolding. "You stick to your type and don't try to write love poems," he said. "You'll never amount to anything as a poet!"

Some time later, Orion had to go out of town on business. Sammy was left to run the newspaper by himself. Nothing interesting had happened in Hannibal recently and Sammy did not know what to put in the newspaper. Finally he got a bright idea.

"I will write some funny stories about the other newspaper editor and draw some pictures to go with them," he planned. "Everybody likes funny stories even if they don't like poems."

Sammy wrote the stories about the other editor and drew pictures to go with them. When the stories were published, everybody who read them laughed and talked about them.

More and more new subscribers came in to subscribe to the *Courier*. The office was filled with more potatoes, beans, and pumpkins than the Clemens family could eat in weeks.

Still Orion was not pleased with Sammy's efforts. "You will get us into trouble," he complained. "That editor is very angry. He may start a fight with me."

"At least that would be exciting to put in the paper," replied Sammy.

Sammy wrote two more poems, but he did not print them in the *Courier*. He sent them away to a magazine which printed them. Sammy did not get any money for the poems, but he was very proud of them just the same.

Orion did not do as well with the newspaper as he had hoped. He had one piece of bad luck after another. One night a cow got into the printing office and ate most of the rubber roller on the press. This was very discouraging to the young editors of the *Courier*.

Orion became cross and faultfinding with Sammy, and the cub printer became restless and unhappy. He spent more and more time down by the river, watching the boats and wishing that he could go away.

"I do not want to spend my life in this sleepy little town," Sammy thought. "I do not want to be a printer. I want to go on the river and be a steamboat pilot. Steamboat men are kings!"

Even though he was unhappy as a printer, Sammy worked hard to help save Orion's newspaper. All the family tried to help. Mrs. Clemens took in boarders and managed to feed them pretty well on her good Southern cooking. They had hot bread dripping with butter, plenty of good country bacon and ham. Many of Orion's customers paid for their subscriptions with produce from their farms, so this was a good way to use the surplus.

Loyal Pamela helped, too. "I'll start a class of music pupils," she said. Many mothers in town were glad to have their children take music lessons from her.

Orion worked desperately, trying everything he could think of to save the paper. Nothing seemed to help. The editorials over which he struggled until late at night were dull.

"If we could only get some interesting stories to run in the paper," said Sammy.

"Good writers won't write stories unless they are paid well," sighed Orion gloomily. He had already written to several authors. None of them was willing to furnish an exciting long serial for a mere five dollars.

A fire broke out in the newspaper office. It did even more damage than the hungry cow had done. Orion got a little insurance money from the fire. In order to save money, he moved the newspaper into the family's house.

Everyone worked together to set up the paper in its new quarters. Orion even built an extra room upstairs, hoping to get more business.

"It's like feeding pain-killer to a dying cat," Orion admitted one day. "I'm not helping any of you and I'm getting as cantankerous as a snapping turtle."

One day Pamela had news for the family. "William Moffett wants me to marry him," she told them. "He is doing well in St. Louis and he says he knows I will be happy there."

William Moffett had been a storekeeper in

Hannibal. He, too, had become restless in the little town. He had always liked the sweet and pretty Pamela and now longed to have her with him. So there was a wedding in the Clemens family and Pamela went off in a big steamboat with her proud and happy husband.

Pamela was radiant as she waved good-by to her family, but there were tears in her eyes, too. She hated to leave the boys. With all her heart she wished she could help her family more.

"We'll miss her, but I'm glad for her," sighed her mother. "She will have a fine home and the good things she deserves."

"And she won't have to worry about money for the next issue of the paper," added Orion. "I'm glad she didn't marry a newspaperman."

Sammy's eyes were wistful as he watched the steamboat disappear. Its harsh whistle was like stirring music to him. At that moment he envied his gentle sister with all his heart.

154

It was not the thought of a fine home, good clothes, and the comfort Pamela would have which thrilled him. The steamboat, gliding along the wide highway of the river represented adventure to him. How he wished he could get onto a boat and follow the river!

Pamela wrote cheerful letters from St. Louis. She invited the family to visit her. She talked of the great opportunities in the city.

"I can't leave my dying cow here in Hannibal," said Orion, referring to his unsuccessful newspaper. "But you, Sammy, might as well hunt for something better."

Sammy realized that his brother was right. He had worked at the newspaper business since he was twelve years old—almost six years now. What did he have to show for it? Nothing but experience. He was now what is called a journeyman printer. He could go any place where newspapers were published and find a job.

The river beckoned and coaxed. "Come on," it seemed to be saying to Sammy. "Follow me. Follow me and see the world!"

One night the moonlight shining through his window wakened him. He noticed that Orion's bed on the other side of the room was empty.

"I suppose he's in the newspaper office trying to write an editorial," thought Sammy. He got out of bed and went into the hot little office with its smell of ink, dust, and paper.

No lamp had been lighted in the room, but the brilliant moonlight showed everything. He saw Orion sitting there in the moonlight.

"I'm thinking, Sammy," said his older brother. "I'm trying to decide something. I've about made up my mind."

Orion told Sammy what he was thinking. Someone had offered to buy the newspaper for five hundred dollars. Orion thought that he would let it go.

"But that's exactly what you owe on the paper," cried Sammy. "That's the exact amount of the mortgage. You wouldn't make a penny."

"I'm not making money now," returned Orion gloomily. "Look Sammy, I'm not even able to pay you the three and a half dollars a week I promised you. And my worries are turning me into a prickly hedgehog."

"I always knew it was the worry talking and not you," said Sammy, who loved his brother dearly. "I didn't really think you hated me."

"But you would come to hate me if you stayed on here," said Orion earnestly. "You'd hate the town. Perhaps you'd even get to hating yourself, like I sometimes do. No, it's time to give up the paper, Sammy."

So the newspaper was sold and the two brothers went adventuring in different ways. Orion went north to Iowa in search of a newspaper which would bring him better luck.

Sammy decided to go to St. Louis. His sister Pamela was delighted to learn that he was coming. She was sure he would soon get a job.

Sammy was looking forward to living and working in the big city. "But St. Louis will be only the first stop in my journey," he promised himself. "I shall see the world and have many adventures."

A Wish Comes True

The day of Sammy's departure arrived. He was very excited as he walked down the street toward the boat landing. He was wearing his best clothes and his hair was neatly brushed.

Mrs. Clemens was walking on one side of him. Orion was on the other. Henry came behind with the carpetbag containing Sammy's clothes.

This was a great day in the life of young Sammy Clemens. He was going away from Hannibal, to the great city of St. Louis down the river to work on another newspaper.

"But I shall not always work on a newspaper," he planned. "When I have saved enough money,

I will use it to take my pilot's training. Then I can be a steamboat pilot!"

"The boat will soon be here, Sammy!" Henry cried excitedly. He pointed toward a gray smoke feather outlined against the sky. "There she comes!"

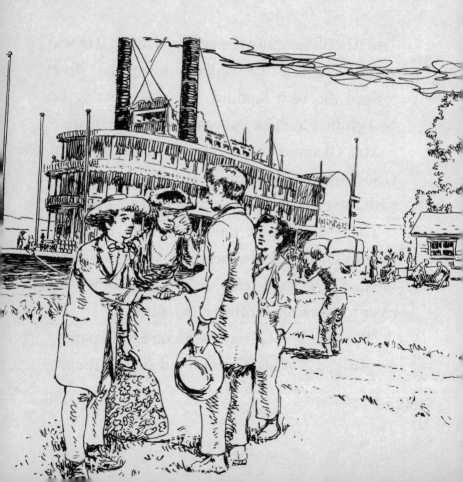

"Good-by, Sammy," said Mrs. Clemens, wiping tears from her eyes with her handkerchief. "Promise me that you will not drink or swear or play cards while you are gone."

Sammy promised. He kept his promise, too.

"Good-by, Sammy," said Orion smiling. "Don't spend too much of your time writing poems and funny stories!"

The two brothers shook hands solemnly. Now that they were saying good-by, they suddenly realized how much they cared for each other. Sammy was sorry he had not worked harder in the newspaper office. Orion felt he had been too cross with his young brother.

"Good-by, Sammy," said Henry. He forgot about all the times he and Sammy had fought and quarreled. "I'll go on a steamboat, too, just as soon as I'm old enough."

A loud hoarse whistle sounded downriver. In a minute the steamboat came into view. Sammy's heart beat fast. How beautiful the great boat looked as it came proudly down the river, water splashing over its wheel!

"Steamboat coming! Steamboat coming!" went up the old cry. This call sent a thrill through Sammy every single time he heard it.

As long as he could remember Sammy had longed to do exactly what he was doing today. He walked across the gangplank onto the deck of the boat. He stood by the rail, waving his hat at his family. He was smiling broadly.

At last the gangplank was lifted. The paddle wheel began to move with a splashing noise through the water. The boat got under way.

"I'm on my way!" whispered Sammy. He watched the shore as the boat traveled along. He could not see his family any more. The little town against the hill grew smaller and smaller.

"I've had a lot of fun there!" he thought. He remembered the times he had played pirate on the island and held meetings with his club in the cave. He thought of Bear Creek and the time he went down there to smoke with Tom.

The little town faded from sight. Gone were the houses, the island, the tiny thread of the creek, the mysterious cave door. Only the tall bluff, crowned with its trees, still showed.

"I'm leaving you!" thought Sammy to himself, "but I'll never forget you!"

He stood up straight and looked at the river he loved so much. The wind blew through his hair and tumbled it. The river spray was like tears on his face.

"Mark Twain, Mark Twain, Mark Twain," sang the paddle wheel, moving faster and faster through the safe, deep water.

"Mark Twain, Mark Twain, Mark Twain," whistled the steam hoarsely.

"Mark Twain, Mark Twain, Mark Twain," echoed the boy. "How I love that sound. It's like a name. I wish it were my name. Mark Twain—safe water. Maybe some day I'll change my name to Mark Twain!"

Sammy smiled at the little joke he was making to himself. He did not know that some day his wish would come true and that he would be called Mark Twain. He did not know that he would become one of the most famous men in America because of the books he would write about his beloved river.

Sammy only knew that he was happy because at last he was riding on a steamboat on the great Mississippi River.

The trip from Hannibal to St. Louis was not a long one. It was too short for Sam Clemens, wild with delight to be riding the breast of the majestic river at last.

He sat on the deck. Thoughts winged through his mind like birds.

"What is the river?" he thought. "Not just a

great stream of water, but many other things as well. What things?"

The steamboat's cat, recognizing a friend, leaped into Sam's lap. He stroked her sweepingly, in time to the words in his thoughts.

"And what is this river?" Sam's thoughts continued. "It is the highway to adventure, the gateway to the world. It has an old, old beauty which never dies. It is an enchanted world of its own with its own islands—loaded rafts moving slowly along its gleaming path.

"Its current is stately, like the step of a king. It is never the same and so it is never dull. Father of rivers, you are more than a river to me. You are my friend, my kinsman!"

Under his stroking hand the cat purred happily and dug gentle claws into his knee. A couple of children strolled by and stopped to exchange greetings with Sam's new-found friend.

"I've never been on a steamboat before," said

the little boy. "It's like fairyland. I wish I could stay the rest of my life. I wouldn't mind if I had to be the boy that scrubs the deck."

Sam Clemens smiled his gentle smile and answered in his pleasant drawling voice, "You and me both, boy. I know just how you feel."

"You wouldn't scrub decks, Gib Miller," said the girl. "You won't even sweep up the floor in Papa's barbershop."

"A barbershop ain't the same thing as a steamboat," said the boy. "And if I could have my ruthers, I'd ruther go on a steamboat than go to Heaven no matter what you say!"

The little girl widened her eyes and looked shocked. "Just wait till Brother Webster hears what you said!" she reproved. She stared at Sam's hair, blown by the river breeze.

"My, you've got a lot of hair!" she said. "It's like a big strawstack, only it's curly. Did you ever take a steamboat trip before?"

166

Sam's smile widened and broke into a lazy, chuckling laugh. His eyes began to sparkle with enjoyment. His ever-ready imagination brightened and flamed.

"Did I ever!" exclaimed Sam. "Why when I was only nine years old I went on the whoppingest steamboat trip you ever heard tell of—just me and my pet frog Ike."

The children gazed wide-eyed. Their attention stirred Sam's imagination even more. "Tell us about it," they begged.

Sam obeyed willingly. He had always loved being the center of attention.

"Well, there was this frog that I had raised from a tadpole," Sam began. "This frog was always wanting to jump into the river. And there were these great grand packet boats going up and down on the river."

Sam told them the story of his stowaway trip that he took when he was nine years old. As he told the story it grew and became more interesting and more exciting.

"That frog became the most amazing frog that ever hatched in a Missouri pond," Sam concluded. "It had the most powerful, high jumping legs ever owned by a frog. Its voice was thunderous. The storm that fell on the packet boat that day was incredibly fierce."

Both story teller and listeners were sorry when the call to eat interrupted their visit.

All too soon for Sam, the voyage came to an end. The steamboat docked at St. Louis. There on the platform was faithful, loving Pamela glowing with joy at seeing her brother. With Pamela was her husband William Moffett.

"There's a job for you in my store, Sam," William Moffett offered, "if you want it. But if you don't I'm sure you can get on the *Evening News*. There's a real future for a newspaperman here in St. Louis."

"I'm so glad you're here, Sammy!" said Pamela squeezing his arm. "Tell me all about everyone at home. Do you have a sweetheart yet? You'll stay with us, won't you?"

Sam had made up his mind about one thing. He felt that his future was not in St. Louis. His future was the wide, wide world. He decided he would stay here just long enough to earn money for further travel.

Into the
Wide World

SAM DID not stay in St. Louis very long. He got
a job on the *Evening News,* but as soon as he
had a little money saved, he took off to see the
world.

First he went to New York City. This was a
thrilling, exciting place for a boy from a small
town like Hannibal.

When Sam arrived in the big city there was a
great fair, called the Crystal Palace Fair, going
on. A special building, the Crystal Palace, had
been built on one end of the island. This made
it seem like a fairyland to Sam.

He wandered through the enchantments of

this palace and wrote long letters back home about the wonderful things he saw.

New York was an exciting place, but Sam got a little homesick. He missed his mother's good southern cooking.

"We never have hot cornbread or biscuits," he complained. "These New York people eat only cold light bread, and if it is stale they like it all the better."

Sam found a job in a printing office in New York where he earned four dollars a week. He managed to save a little from his earnings, and often had fifty cents a week left over.

Sam discovered one place in New York which was a real treasure-trove to him.

"Imagine," he wrote to Pamela, "only a short walk from my boarding house is a free printers' library. It contains more than 4,000 volumes. I spend my evenings wandering among those treasures. The evenings are never long enough!"

Pamela read this part of Sam's letter over several times.

"Sammy is growing up," she told her husband. "Think of it, William, he hated school   He was a real failure with all his teachers. And our parents worried for fear he would grow up into a dunce!

"I always had faith in Sammy," she added fondly. "I knew he would do something special when he grew up."

"He's not really grown-up yet," the merchant said to his wife kindly. "He's just beginning to sprout his wing feathers."

"My future is in the wide world," Sam had said. Soon he left New York and went on to Philadelphia. He visited the grave of Benjamin Franklin and his wife, Deborah.

"His future was the wide world, too," thought the young printer. He pondered long about the life of the great man who was buried here.

"We're alike in lots of ways," Sam thought. "Both of us started out as printers. Each worked for an older brother and began writing little poems and articles for a newspaper. We both became traveling printers, never settling in one place, but journeying about."

There was still another way in which the two might be alike. The young man felt strangely excited as he stood by the tomb of the old man who had filled a long life with greatness.

"I have a long way to go yet," Sam thought. He was glad he was young and vigorous.

He was now a journeyman printer and the name suited him well, for he was constantly journeying. He journeyed among the big cities —New York, Philadelphia, Washington.

When he got homesick for his family he journeyed back to St. Louis to visit Pamela. Then he went on to a town in Iowa where Orion had bought another newspaper.

Orion was married now. Henry was working for Orion as Sam once had.

Sam stayed and worked a while there. Everybody was glad to have him, for he was full of fun and good spirits. Life seemed more interesting when he was around.

Whenever Sam became restless, as he often did, he would take off again to another city. Usually he would travel somewhere by boat either on the Ohio or Mississippi River. He preferred the Mississippi, because it was larger and went farther than the Ohio.

One April day, Sam went down to the river. He was feeling restless. Once more he had that old yearning to travel on a boat.

"I'd like to travel down the Mississippi River and on to the Amazon River in South America," Sam thought to himself. "I bet the Amazon's a real river."

As usual Sam acted first and thought afterwards. A boat bound for New Orleans was getting ready to pull away from the dock. He got on board. He waited till the boat was well under way and walked into the pilot house.

"Do you need a young man to learn the river?" he asked the captain.

Captain Bixby looked up in surprise. He had not thought of taking on a cub pilot, but Sam had a way with people. He had the great gift of likability.

Besides that, Captain Bixby had a sore foot that day. So when Sam said that he knew how to steer a steamboat, the captain was glad for the chance to take a short rest.

That was an important ride. The captain agreed to take on the young man as a learner. Of course Sam would have to pay five hundred dollars for the training. He did not have five hundred dollars, but William Moffett did. He was willing to advance the money to Sam.

Thus Sam started on the career about which he had dreamed all his life. Forgotten were his ambitions to be a printer, or a writer, or even a newspaper publisher.

Nothing had ever seemed so glorious as steaming along the river and into some crowded port. Those were the days when the steamboat was the king of travel.

The city levees were thrilling places. The waterfront was always crowded with drays, trucks, and great piles of produce. Steamboats stood side by side in the water, their tall smoke-stacks puffing gently. Sometimes there was a line of boats a mile long. It was glorious to be a part of that stately parade.

The pilot house in a big steamboat was high above the water. When Sam stood behind the wheel of a stately craft like the "Paul Jones," he felt a tremendous thrill.

"Steamboat men are kings!" he used to say when he was a little boy, wistfully watching the packets at Hannibal.

He still thought that steamboat men were kings. "And I feel like a king!" he murmured.

Sam didn't care whether he ever got to the Amazon River now or not. This one was good enough for him!

Horace Bixby was a good teacher. He was good in more ways than one. He not only taught Sam piloting, but he taught him to keep careful notes, too. He taught Sam to know the river as he would know his own yard at home.

Sam was a good scholar. He got a notebook and soon filled it with the name of every bend, bar, island, town, settlement, and shore.

"I never saw a cub pilot learn the river any better than you," Captain Bixby praised him. "You've got a natural gift for it."

"That's because I love the river more than anything in the world," replied Sam fervently. "I've always loved the river, even from the time I was a toddler back in Missouri."

A MERRY PART IN THE WORLD

Sam Clemens had time for thinking as he stood at his pilot wheel. Sometimes he thought of things he had read—history, Bible stories, poetry, and novels.

He often thought of authors whose books he

had enjoyed reading. He wondered what kind of men they really were.

"Edgar Allan Poe had a sad life," Sam recalled. "His mind was haunted, like an old deserted house. And Charles Dickens, what a climb up in the world he made. I guess he was the greatest lecturer that ever lived!"

Sam had put aside his literary ambitions for a while. But he kept careful notebooks of his river knowledge. Sometimes he wrote down his thoughts about life and his future.

"What will the future bring?" he sometimes wondered. For though he loved steamboat piloting, he knew the time would come when he must go on and learn more of the world.

One day he wrote down some of his thoughts about life. He was not sure whether they were thoughts he had read somewhere, or thoughts which had come to him. But they expressed what he felt and he remembered them.

"Take life as though it was earnest and vital and important," he wrote. "Live it as if you were born to the task of performing a merry part in it. Act as though the world had waited your coming and welcomed you here. Live as if life was a grand opportunity to do and achieve and carry on great plans. Be on the lookout to help and cheer a suffering, weary, and maybe a heartbroken brother."

These were some of the lines which Sam put down in his little notebook. They were a very good set of rules for any young man to steer his life by.

"Live life—really live it." These five words might have been his motto as the years of his life went on.

His life as a steamboat pilot ended when Fort Sumter was fired on in 1861. Sam Clemens became a soldier, then a pioneer to the far west state of Nevada.

After that he became a prospector for gold and silver, then a miner. Finally he went back to his old job of newspaper work. He began working on a paper called the *Enterprise* in the town of Virginia City, Nevada.

Sam was now twenty-seven years old. Many people have found their place in the world at that age, but Sam was still learning. Everything that he had done in his life up to now were helping him to learn.

His steamboat experience had taught him to remember and to keep careful notes. His reading, back in the East, had given him a great knowledge of history and poetry.

Working on the different newspapers had taught Sam how to report happenings. He had always loved the sound of words and phrases, even as a very small child.

Out here in the West things were happening, and happening fast. History was being made.

Sam wrote articles about the mining state and the exciting things that went on there. People liked his articles for they were lively, interesting, and often very funny.

Sam decided that he wanted to have a name signed to his writings. He did not wish to write newspaper stories without a name.

"I must think of a good pen name," he said to his editor one day.

In those days most authors used what they called a pen name. They did not sign their own names to their writings.

"What do you want to call yourself?" asked the editor curiously.

It did not take Sam very long to decide. His pen name must have some connection with the river he had always loved.

"Mark Twain. That's it, Mark Twain!" Sam replied jubilantly. How often he had rejoiced to hear the sound of those words.

"Mark Twain" meant safe water.

People liked Mark Twain's articles. They were lively, interesting, funny, and packed full of enjoyment.

"People like to laugh," said one of Sam's friends. His friend's pen name was Artemus Ward. "Laughing is good for them. You're a natural born humorist, Sam. You must never stop writing."

Artemus Ward was a humorist, too. "But you are far better now than I shall ever be," he told Mark Twain.

So Mark Twain kept writing. He kept traveling and seeing the world, too.

He traveled to California where he wrote a book called, *The Jumping Frog of Calaveras County*. Perhaps he remembered Ike, his first steamboat companion, as he wrote it.

He found out that writing was not his only talent. People liked to hear him speak. Even when he was working for Orion back in Keokuk, he would sometimes give a talk at a dinner. Those talks by Sam Clemens were always the most enjoyable part of the dinner.

Now he discovered that he could talk to a large crowd of people in a hall. He would tell them about his experiences. The people would flock to hear him wherever he lectured.

"He's better than Charles Dickens ever was," some of the oldtimers said.

Sam traveled to the Mediterranean and the Holy Land. Now he was thankful for those long ago Sunday school lessons in Hannibal.

Life was busy and crowded for Mark Twain. He traveled a great deal and saw much of the world. He kept careful notes of all he saw. Some of his notes were used for the lectures which were so popular. Some grew into books.

One Christmastime Sam went to New York to spend the holiday with friends. While he was there they all went to hear the famous Charles Dickens give one of his lectures.

In the theater party were the Langdon family. With them was their lovely daughter Olivia.

Sam had looked forward to hearing this famous author and lecturer, but he did not remember very much about Mr. Dickens. All he could think of was Olivia, who sat beside him.

Now Sam had a new ambition.

"I'm going to marry Olivia," he resolved.

Olivia was a lovely, delicate young woman, who had been hurt in a fall several years before. She was still very fragile.

"But Olivia is the woman I want for my wife," thought the adventurous, daring, fun-loving young man. "I shall marry her."

So Sam and Olivia were married, and she was a great help to him in his work. She read all his writings carefully and corrected all the errors which she found.

Sam's pet name for her was Livy. She called him Youth.

Other books began to take their places along side of *The Jumping Frog*. Most of them grew out of things that had happened to Mark Twain.

As he looked back on his childhood days at Hannibal, it seemed to him that those were the most glorious days of his life. They shimmered with the wonderful magic of happy memory.

"I want to capture the happiness of being a boy in a river town," he resolved, "and keep it for boys in all the world."

That is exactly what Mark Twain did when he wrote his book *Huckleberry Finn.* This book has been a favorite with boys and girls since it was first published in 1884.

The Famous
Mark Twain

As THE YEARS went by more and more people began to hear about the great writer and humorist Mark Twain. More and more people wondered about this man who wrote books that everybody loved to read.

"Mark Twain—isn't he that little towheaded Sammy Clemens who used to live here?" the people around Hannibal asked each other.

Yes, they all soon learned that the great Mark Twain, the man who was honored wherever he went, was none other than mischievous little Sammy Clemens.

Sammy kept the promise he made to himself

when he took the steamboat to St. Louis those many years ago. He never forgot Hannibal where he grew up, nor did he forget Uncle John's farm, nor the gang of boys with whom he had played.

Mark Twain wrote about them all in his books. He wrote about the fun he and his gang had had in the cave, on the river, and up the hill. He wrote so well that people who read his books and stories feel they are living in that same little town by the great Mississippi.

Today, if you should visit Hannibal, Missouri, you would see many things to remind you of how much the people love Mark Twain's books.

There are highways and streets named for him throughout the state. The cave where he and his club once pretended to be pirates is now called "Mark Twain's Cave."

The house where he lived as a child is carefully kept and many visitors go through it each

MARK TWAIN-

day. A statue of him stands on the hill behind the house where he once played.

In another part of town there is also a statue of two boys. They appear to be about eleven years old. One of the boys carries a fishing rod, and the other is holding a dead cat.

"That statue is a statue of Tom Sawyer and Huckleberry Finn," people say. "The best books Mark Twain ever wrote were about those two boys and their adventures."

Tom Sawyer and Huckleberry Finn are the names Mark Twain gave to himself and his old friend Tom Blankenship in his books.

Mark Twain wrote an exciting book about his adventures as a steamboat pilot called *Life on the Mississippi*. Nobody else has ever written about the great river and the river towns as well as Mark Twain wrote about them.

Many people call the Mississippi River, "Mark Twain's river," because he wrote such good stories about it. He would be very happy to know that, for more than anything in the world, he loved the great river.

Late in life Mark Twain lost all his money trying to publish his own books. He also invested money in a typesetting machine which proved unsuccessful. Both ventures created many debts, debts which he was determined to pay. To do this he started out to earn money by a lecture tour of the world.

The tour was so successful that Mark Twain was able to pay every debt. Having accomplished this, he lived in New York City for a time. Later he moved to Redding, Connecticut, where he died on April 21, 1910.